"Layla will be sorry she missed you," Reese told Michael.

"She's eaten at your restaurant several times, but she's never had the pleasure of meeting you."

"How long will she be gone?" Michael asked.

"Two months."

A wolfish gleam filled his dark eyes. "So we've got the place to ourselves…all night long."

Reese felt a quiver of anticipation at his words and the deep, seductive timbre of his voice. Holding his gaze, she softly repeated, "All night long."

That was all the invitation Michael needed.

Before Reese could react, Michael grabbed her into his arms, bringing her flush against his hard, powerful body. Her breath momentarily stopped and her heart rate tripled. As she stared up into his eyes, he framed her face between his big hands and slanted his mouth hungrily over hers. Pleasure exploded in her veins. She wrapped her arms around his neck, melting against him with a low moan.

His lips were even softer than she'd imagined, moving sensually over hers. The taste and heat of his body were unbearably arousing as he eased his tongue into her mouth slowly, deeply. She opened to him, shaking so hard she could barely stand. He wrapped one of his arms around her, holding her so tightly their bodies could have been joined.

She didn't realize he was backing her up until she felt the wooden edge of the sideboard against her backside. Michael lifted her with astonishing ease and set her down on the table. Reese clung to his broad shoulders as he took her mouth again in another deep, smoldering kiss.

Books by Maureen Smith

Kimani Romance

A Legal Affair
A Guilty Affair
Secret Agent Seduction
Touch of Heaven
Recipe for Temptation

Kimani Arabesque

With Every Breath
A Heartbeat Away

MAUREEN SMITH

is the author of fourteen novels and one novella. She received a B.A. in English from the University of Maryland with a minor in creative writing. She is a former freelance writer; her articles have been featured in various print and online publications. Since the publication of her debut novel in 2002, Maureen has been nominated for three *RT Book Reviews* Reviewers' Choice Awards and twelve Emma Awards, and she has won the *Romance in Color* Reviewers' Choice Awards for New Author of the Year and Romantic Suspense of the Year.

Maureen currently lives in San Antonio, Texas, with her husband, two children and a miniature schnauzer. She loves to hear from readers and can be reached at author@maureen-smith.com. Please visit her Web site at www.maureen-smith.com for news about her upcoming releases.

Recipe for
TEMPTATION

MAUREEN SMITH

To the wonderful ladies of my Yahoo group,
who have been faithfully staking their claim to the
"Wolf Pack" for years

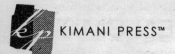 KIMANI PRESS™

ISBN-13: 978-0-373-86167-5

Recycling programs
for this product may
not exist in your area.

RECIPE FOR TEMPTATION

www.kimanipress.com

Printed in U.S.A.

Dear Reader,

In 2006 you were introduced to Michael Wolf in my novel *Taming the Wolf*. Since then, I have received an outpouring of e-mails from readers whose hearts were stolen by the sexy, charming chef. Once I decided to give Michael his own story—really, I had no other choice—my next big task was to find the right woman for him. I likened it to being a casting director in search of the perfect actress to share the silver screen with a popular leading man.

I scoured my imagination day and night, searching for the woman who would heat up more than Michael's gourmet kitchen. And then—bam!—along came Reese St. James from *Touch of Heaven*. She was perfect in every way. And you know what? I hope you'll think so, too!

As always, please share your thoughts with me at author@maureen-smith.com.

Until next time, happy reading and *bon appétit!*

Maureen Smith

ACKNOWLEDGMENTS

My utmost gratitude to Tanisha Holmes,
who graciously took me on a "virtual tour"
of the beautiful, lively city of Atlanta.

A very special thanks to Dr. Keisha Loftin, who took
time out of her busy schedule to answer my questions
about medical procedure, and to Sylvia Hightower, R.N.,
whose heartrending experiences in an operating room
helped bring my prologue to life.

And a heartfelt thank-you to my editor, Kelli Martin,
who patiently brainstormed with me and helped whip
this book into shape.

Prologue

May 2010
Houston, Texas

"Time of death." Dr. Reese St. James glanced up at the clock hung on the east wall of the operating room. "Nine thirty-four."

A somber hush fell upon the room.

The medical personnel gathered around the operating table watched as Reese slowly pulled the sheet over Deidra Thomas's lifeless face.

Reese couldn't believe her patient was gone. It seemed impossible, like a horrific nightmare from which she would soon awaken.

Everything had happened so quickly. One minute Reese had been performing a routine cesarean section on Deidra Thomas. The next minute the woman was coding, in the throes of sudden cardiac arrest. Pandemonium had erupted in the operating room as Reese and her colleagues raced to save both mother and child.

But it was too late for Deidra.

A hard lump of sorrow rose in Reese's throat. Her gaze traveled across the room to where the pediatric surgeon, flanked by two nurses, was tending to the newborn. Feeling as though she was in a trance, Reese walked over to the warmer to get a better look at the baby girl she'd just delivered.

She was flailing her tiny arms and wailing in protest of being poked, weighed and measured. But as Reese approached, the infant turned her head and eyed her curiously. Reese's throat tightened when she saw that the baby had inherited her mother's almond-shaped brown eyes and dimpled chin.

Reese smiled tenderly. "Hello, Faith."

The newborn grew silent, gazing alertly at her.

The attending pediatrician glanced up from his patient to look at Reese. Above his surgical mask, his green eyes were kind and sympathetic. "She's going to be fine, Reese," he assured her. "She's perfectly healthy."

Reese nodded, swallowing with difficulty. "I have to go… tell her father."

The pediatrician nodded. As Reese turned away, he gave her shoulder a gentle squeeze.

With slow, painstaking precision, Reese removed her blood-stained surgical gown, gloves and mask, then dropped the soiled items into the biohazard waste container near the double doors. Raw emotion was clawing at her throat, choking her, but outwardly she remained calm and composed. She had to. She was a professional. So she had to forget that Deidra Thomas was the first patient she'd ever had. She had to forget that she'd delivered all of Deidra's babies. She had to forget that Deidra and her family held a special place in her heart.

Drawing a deep breath, Reese left the operating room and started down the brightly lit corridor on leaden legs.

Ian Thomas was anxiously pacing back and forth in the waiting room. He'd been at his wife's bedside when she began seizing. For as long as Reese lived, she would never forget the sound of his panicked shouts as he was hastily removed from the operating room.

He glanced up now as Reese approached. He took one look at her face and began shaking his head in vehement denial. "No. No. *Nooo!*"

Reese gently explained, "Deidra had an amniotic fluid embolism, Mr. Thomas. It's a rare disorder where amniotic fluid enters the mother's bloodstream, causing the heart and lungs to collapse. We did everything we—"

"No. This can't be happening." Ian Thomas's face contorted with anguished grief. "Please God… Not my Deidra. *Not my Deidra!*"

Reese's heart constricted in her chest. Tears burned her eyes. Yet all she could say was, "I'm so sorry."

Chapter 1

Two months later
Atlanta, Georgia

"Ma'am? This is your stop."

Reese blinked, dazedly staring out the window of the taxicab she'd taken into Midtown Atlanta that evening. She couldn't believe she'd already reached her destination. She'd meant to take in the sights and sounds of the bustling metropolis during the cab ride into town. Instead she'd zoned out, succumbing to painful memories of the day her patient died in childbirth.

Deidra Thomas's untimely death had left her husband and family reeling with shock and grief. Although Reese had tried her damnedest to distance herself emotionally from the tragedy, every time she closed her eyes at night, she saw Ian Thomas's ravaged face, heard his anguished wails of denial. Every time Reese delivered a new baby, she was gripped by a terrible fear that something would go wrong. She was losing sleep, becoming withdrawn and finding it difficult to concentrate at work, which was not only unfair to her patients, but dangerous, as well.

And then one day out of the blue, she'd received a phone call from her longtime friend Layla Chase. An award-winning photojournalist for *National Geographic,* Layla had mentioned that she was looking for someone to house-sit for her while she was on assignment in Somalia for two months. Almost immediately Reese had known that this was the lifeline she'd so desperately needed, an opportunity to take a sabbatical before she had a nervous breakdown. She'd made the arrangements with Layla, cleared her leave of absence with the hospital, then packed her bags and headed to Atlanta.

She'd made a pact with herself not to discuss or even *think* about work for the next two months. Yet there she was, torturing herself with thoughts of Deidra Thomas and the motherless children she'd left behind.

"Ma'am? Are you okay?"

Reese glanced up, embarrassed to realize that the cabdriver had opened the back door and was patiently waiting for her to get out so he could be on his way.

Glancing quickly at the electronic meter, Reese fished three twenties out of her Louis Vuitton handbag and passed the money to the cabbie. "Keep the change," she told him as she climbed out of the taxi.

He beamed at her. "Thank you, ma'am. Enjoy your dinner. You can't go wrong with anything on the menu."

"So I've heard," Reese said with a smile.

As she joined the flow of patrons heading into the brick-fronted restaurant, she couldn't help feeling a thrill of excitement. For the past three years she'd dreamed of visiting Wolf's Soul, a world-renowned restaurant made famous by owner and executive chef Michael Wolf. Reese, whose favorite hobby was cooking, had been a huge fan of the hunky celebrity chef ever since he burst onto the national scene with his cable television show *Howlin' Good.* Reese owned all four of his bestselling cookbooks, religiously TiVoed his program and had prepared many of his recipes for her family and friends, who often teased her about having the hots for the popular chef. Not that anyone in their right mind could blame her. With his dark good looks and smoldering charisma, Michael Wolf had stolen the hearts of women everywhere, solidifying his status as a bona fide sex symbol.

Located just a few blocks from the Fox Theatre in Midtown Atlanta, Wolf's Soul boasted a clientele that included famous celebrities, athletes and politicians whose images were captured in framed photographs that graced the mahogany-paneled walls. Over the years Michael Wolf had hosted everyone who was anyone—from movie mogul Tyler Perry to President Barack Obama, who'd made a stop at the restaurant during the historic election campaign two years ago.

As Reese waited in line to be seated, she wondered if she'd be lucky enough to catch a glimpse of Michael Wolf tonight. Despite his busy schedule—which included the daily taping of his show, book signings and regular visits to his six other restaurants scattered around the country—he still managed to put in several hours a week at the Atlanta location whenever he was in town. As luck would have it, she'd heard on the radio that morning that he'd just returned from a national media tour to begin taping the new season of *Howlin' Good*. After years of admiring him from afar, the possibility of seeing Michael Wolf in person filled Reese with giddy anticipation. She'd even brought a copy of his very first cookbook in the hopes of getting his autograph.

As the maître d' escorted Reese to her table, she eagerly took in her surroundings. With the restaurant's high ceilings and recessed lights turned strategically low, she felt as if she were entering the heart of a plush cave. The tables were made of gleaming mahogany and accentuated with soft candlelight. Music floated from a baby grand piano tucked into a shadowy corner, subtle enough to add to the intimate ambiance without drowning out the pleasant buzz of laughter and conversation.

Reese was led to a small table in a private corner that gave her an unobstructed view of the entire dining room, which was perfect. She could enjoy her meal and people-watch in peace.

After she was seated, the maître d' passed her a leather-bound menu and a thick wine list. Almost at once, a waiter appeared to fill her water glass and drape a linen napkin across her lap.

After placing her order, Reese glanced around the restaurant. Even on a Tuesday night the place was packed, every table and booth occupied. Reese made eye contact with an attractive stranger seated alone at a nearby table. He smiled invitingly and raised his glass in a toast to her. She returned his smile before glancing away.

She hadn't come to Atlanta looking for romance. In fact, romance was the *last* thing on her mind these days. For the past year she'd been dating one of her colleagues at the hospital, a cardiothoracic surgeon named Victor Carracci. Handsome, intelligent and incredibly gifted, Victor was everything Reese could ever want in a man. From the very beginning he'd wined and dined her and made her laugh. Yet something was still missing between them.

It didn't help that over the past few months she'd sensed a growing distance between them. She told herself that their busy careers were putting a strain on their relationship, but deep down inside she knew that their problems were more complicated than conflicting schedules.

Before leaving Houston, she'd suggested to Victor that they use the time apart from each other to figure out what they both wanted. He'd agreed, but not without first telling her that she couldn't solve her problems by running away.

The waiter returned at that moment, interrupting Reese's grim musings. She took a grateful sip of wine, then dug into the steaming lobster bisque. It was delicious. She ate slowly, savoring each spoonful.

Halfway through dinner, her cell phone rang. Reluctantly she reached inside her handbag and checked caller ID. She frowned when she saw Victor's number. She'd barely been gone two days. He'd promised to give her time to settle in before he called her.

Damn it, Reese thought as she turned off the phone and resumed eating. She wasn't ready to talk to Victor. Not yet. Maybe not for a while.

"I hope that frown has nothing to do with what's on your plate," said a deep, masculine voice laced with Southern heat.

Reese's head snapped up.

Her breath stalled in her lungs.

Staring down at her was a pair of dark, mesmerizing eyes set in an arrestingly handsome face. A face she recognized immediately.

"Michael Wolf." His name escaped in a throaty whisper of awe.

A hint of a smile curved lush, sensual lips that promised untold delights. "At your service," he drawled.

Reese gulped, heart hammering against her ribs. She couldn't believe it. Michael Wolf was actually standing at her table and speaking to her!

She'd always imagined that when—and *if*—this moment ever came, she wouldn't be reduced to a fawning idiot. Nope, not her. She'd be the epitome of calm, cool and collected. She'd be charming and witty, impressing Michael with clever little anecdotes that demonstrated her own culinary prowess.

But when she opened her mouth to speak, what came out was a breathy "I'm one of your biggest fans."

Those dark, penetrating eyes glittered with amusement. "Is that right?"

Reese instantly wanted to duck under the table. What the hell was wrong with her? She'd graduated at the top of her class from a prestigious medical school. She was a respected obstetrician who'd given lectures to some of the best minds in medicine. She was a smart, confident, articulate woman. Yet all she could come up with was a lame *I'm one of your biggest fans?*

So much for not being reduced to a fawning idiot.

Michael gave her a slow, lazy smile that tripled her heart rate. "I just stopped by to see if you were enjoying your meal."

"Oh, yes. Absolutely. Everything is delicious."

"Good. Glad to hear it."

After following his career and fantasizing about him for so long, Reese couldn't believe she was finally face-to-face with Michael Wolf. She'd always thought he was good-looking on television, but *nothing* compared to seeing him up close and personal. Her hungry gaze swiftly catalogued smooth mahogany skin, low-cut black hair, heavy eyebrows and chiseled cheekbones. His nose was strong and masculine, and his firm chin hinted at a cleft that was indescribably sexy. He was tall, with shoulders as wide as a mountain range and a ruggedly powerful build to match. He wore a black Armani tuxedo with the silk tie hanging loose around his collar, as if he'd yanked it free the first chance he got. No television camera could begin to capture the overwhelming virility of the man, a raw animal magnetism he exuded like a potent drug.

Reese couldn't take her eyes off him. And it wasn't lost on her that Michael seemed in no particular hurry to move on to the next table. His dark eyes traced her features in a slow, deliberate perusal that elevated her blood pressure. When his gaze drifted to her cleavage and lingered, her breasts swelled to aching. She was afraid to look down and see her nipples saluting him through the lightweight sarong dress she wore.

"Is this your first time here?" Michael asked, returning his attention to her face.

"Yes." *But it definitely won't be my last!*

"How long have you been in town?"

"Two days." Reese gave him a saucy smile. "How did you know I was from out of town?"

Michael chuckled softly. "We've been open for seven years. If you were really one of my biggest fans and you lived in Atlanta, it wouldn't have taken you this long to visit the restaurant."

Her smile widened. "Good point."

They stared at each other. The voltage between them scorched her nerve endings and left her feeling hot and tingly all over.

"Well," Michael murmured, "I'll let you get back to your dinner."

Reese felt a sharp pang of disappointment. She didn't want him to leave. There was no guarantee she'd ever see him in person again.

Before she could stop herself, she blurted, "Why don't you join me?"

He looked at her, a smile lurking in one corner of his mouth. If he was surprised by her invitation, he didn't show it. No doubt he was used to strange women throwing themselves at him.

"I already had dinner," he told her, lips quirking.

Reese boldly held his gaze. "Then keep me company until I finish mine."

Something hot and wicked flared in his eyes. "With pleasure."

As he lowered his long, powerful body into a chair, she caught the subtle, masculine spice of an expensive cologne. She couldn't help noticing that every eye in the restaurant was trained on them, as if a spotlight were beaming down on their table. Several women were glaring enviously at Reese, making her glad that looks couldn't kill.

"What's your poison?" Michael asked, nodding toward her half-empty glass.

"Riesling," she answered.

With the barest hint of a nod, he signaled to her waiter, who must have been standing at the ready. A bottle of Riesling was produced within moments.

"Wow," Reese said after the young waiter had topped off her glass and glided away. "You didn't even have to crook a finger. I'm impressed."

Michael chuckled softly. "I take good care of my employees. They like to return the favor. Finish your food before it gets cold."

"Yes, sir." Smiling, Reese picked up her fork and continued eating. "This stuffed salmon is to die for."

"I'm glad you like it," Michael stated, leaning back comfortably in his chair. "It's one of my favorite dishes on the menu."

Reese gave him a teasing, hopeful grin. "Any chance you could share the recipe?"

"That depends." There was a wolfish gleam in his eyes. "What would I get in return?"

Heat rushed into Reese's belly. She stared at him, the air between them vibrating with sexual awareness. For several moments she forgot how to breathe, let alone speak.

"Well?" Michael prompted at length. "What would I get in return for giving you the recipe to one of my prized signature dishes?"

Reese smiled slowly. "My undying gratitude?"

Michael laughed, a low, husky rumble that made her nipples tighten. God, he was sexy. Sexier than any mortal man had a right to be. "And here I thought you'd promise to write a glowing review of the restaurant or something," he teased.

Reese guffawed. "You already have a ton of those. What difference would mine make?"

Before he could respond, they were interrupted by two attractive black women, each bearing a copy of Michael's latest bestselling cookbook.

"Excuse us, Mr. Wolf," gushed the taller of the pair. "We couldn't wait for you to make your way over to our table. May we have your autograph?"

"Of course," Michael answered smoothly, standing to greet the women like the Southern gentleman he was.

As he signed each of their books, they raved about his show and told him how much they'd always enjoyed eating at his restaurant, which they declared to be the best in all of Georgia. He took their compliments in stride, smiling and conversing with them with a lazy charm that Reese found utterly disarming.

At one point, the taller woman whipped out her cell phone

and turned to Reese with a giddy smile. "Would you mind taking a picture of us with Michael?"

"Not at all," Reese said.

She snapped a group photo, then two more as each woman insisted on posing alone with Michael.

After they left—with obvious reluctance—Reese said to Michael, "I've kept you from the rest of your customers. I'm sorry."

His eyes glinted. "Are you?"

She paused. "Not really."

They smiled at each other. The moment stretched into two.

Dragging her gaze away, Reese returned her attention to her plate. "So," she began idly, "do you always come to the restaurant dressed in a tux?"

Michael glanced down at himself, as if he'd forgotten what he was wearing. "I was at a fundraiser dinner. I decided to stop by the restaurant on my way home." His voice deepened as he stared at her. "I'm glad I did."

Reese felt herself blushing like a schoolgirl. "So am I."

His mouth curved with a slow, sexy smile. "What brings you to Atlanta, Miss—?"

"St. James." Reese took a long sip of wine. No way was she telling him about the devastating tragedy that had sent her fleeing to Atlanta. He didn't need to hear about her personal problems.

Smiling demurely, she said, "What if I told you that I came to Atlanta just to eat at your fine establishment?"

Michael chuckled softly. "I suppose I'd be flattered. If I actually believed you."

"You should. I'm one of your biggest fans, remember?"

"Of course. How could I forget?"

They exchanged playful grins.

Finished with her meal, Reese sat back in her chair with a deep, satisfied sigh. "That was heavenly."

"Ready for dessert?" Michael asked.

Only if you're on the menu!

Aloud she said laughingly, "I don't know if I have any room left. I'm stuffed."

"Come on. You can't leave my restaurant without trying one of our amazing desserts."

Of course, Reese needed little convincing.

On cue, the waiter materialized with the dessert menu.

"What do you recommend?" Reese asked Michael.

He smiled. "I think everything's good, but of course I'm biased. Why don't you try the sweet potato pecan pie?"

Reese smiled. "Sounds good."

As the waiter bustled away, Michael shook his head slowly at Reese. "Dangerous," he murmured.

"What?"

"Your smile. It's a heartbreaker."

Reese laughed, even as her stomach bottomed out. "I bet you say that to all the girls."

"No," he said softly, "just you."

They gazed at each other.

If someone had told Reese that on her second night in Atlanta she'd find herself seated at a cozy dinner table with America's sexiest chef—as Michael had recently been dubbed by *People* magazine—she wouldn't have believed it. Not in a million years. She wanted to pinch herself just to make sure she wasn't dreaming.

But, no, this moment *had* to be real. Michael Wolf sat close enough for her to see the thick, spiky lashes that rimmed his dark eyes. Close enough for her to detect the beginnings of a five o'clock shadow darkening his jaw. Close enough for her to reach out and touch him—if she dared.

Before she could even think about working up the nerve, her dessert arrived. She let out an involuntary gasp when she saw the enormous slice of pie on her plate. "Oh my God."

"Something wrong?" Michael sounded amused.

"There's no way I can eat all this by myself." She gave him a beseeching look. "You have to help me."

He chuckled. "I don't think—"

"No, really, I insist. Can you bring another fork for your boss?" she asked the waiter.

After another set of silverware had been supplied, Reese pushed the pie plate to the center of the table, and she and Michael dug in.

"Mmmm," she said appreciatively after her first bite. "Delicious."

"You like?"

"Mmm-hmm. You are looking at one *very* satisfied customer."

"That's good," Michael drawled, gazing at her. "Your satisfaction is our number-one priority."

Reese's pulse thudded. The dark, intoxicating timbre of his voice had her imagining a number of other ways *he* could satisfy her. Ways that had nothing whatsoever to do with food.

As if Michael had read her mind, a shadow of a smile lifted the corners of his mouth. He ate another forkful of pie and chewed slowly, watching her. Transfixed, she stared at his full lips, wondering if they were as soft as they looked, wondering how exquisite they'd feel pressed against her mouth, wrapped around a taut nipple, sliding up her inner thigh toward her—

"I know we just met," Michael said quietly, interrupting her lascivious thoughts, "but I was wondering if I could call you sometime?"

"I'd like that," Reese responded, surprising herself. "In fact, if you're free tonight, I could use a ride home."

Chapter 2

Michael didn't make a habit of picking up women at his restaurant—though not for lack of opportunities. In the seven years he'd been in business, he'd received more than his fair share of propositions from customers. Some were subtle, while others…not so much. He'd had half-naked women sneak into the kitchen where he was cooking, while others had tried to bribe his waiters into divulging his home address and phone number.

Yeah, Michael was no stranger to getting hit on. But he'd never believed in using any of his restaurants as his own personal hunting ground.

Until he saw *her*.

The moment he'd stepped into the crowded dining room that evening, his gaze had been drawn to a lone woman seated at a table in a private corner of the restaurant. Flawless deep brown skin gleamed under the recessed lighting. Layers of sleek black hair framed dark cat eyes, high cheekbones and lush, pouty lips that made him envy the fork she was sliding into her mouth. Full, voluptuous breasts beckoned to him from the low neckline of her dress.

Michael had always made a practice of greeting his guests and making them feel at home. But tonight he'd been distracted as he played gracious host, keeping one eye on the exotic mystery woman as he slowly but surely worked his way toward her. When he finally reached her table, she'd looked up at him with those sultry eyes and breathed his name in a siren's voice that sent a bolt of pure lust tearing through his body.

When she'd invited him to join her at the table, refusing her never even entered his mind. He wanted her with a ferocity that had intensified with every seductive smile she gave him, every heated look they'd exchanged.

He wanted her like no other woman he'd ever wanted before.

As luck would have it, she seemed willing to let him have her.

After dinner, she excused herself to use the ladies' room before they left. Michael watched her go, admiring the view of her lushly rounded butt in a white sarong dress that molded every ripe, delectable curve.

Once she'd disappeared from view, he made a beeline for the kitchen to tell his staff he was leaving. As he neared the back foyer he passed Griffin Palmer, the restaurant's maître d'.

"Evening, Griff," he said.

"Evening, boss." Griffin gave him a sly smile. "You and Miss St. James seemed to be getting along rather well."

Michael grinned. "You could say that. She's a beautiful woman."

"That she is." Griffin winked at him. "And I suppose it never hurts to give food critics the VIP treatment. Not that *you* need to bribe anyone into giving the restaurant rave reviews," he added quickly.

Michael stared at him, his grin faltering. "What're you talking about, Griff? Who's a food critic?"

"Miss St. James. She called two weeks ago, said she'd never

been to the restaurant and thought it was high time she paid us a visit." Griffin frowned. "Didn't she introduce herself to you?"

"No."

Once upon a time, food critics had prided themselves on their secrecy. They'd conducted reviews anonymously because they understood the value of experiencing a restaurant just like ordinary patrons. But nowadays, many food critics didn't hesitate to reveal their identities. Michael had trained his staff to treat all customers the same—with warmth, courtesy and respect. He didn't believe in kissing anyone's ass just to get a good review.

"What paper does Miss St. James write for?" he asked Griffin.

"The *Houston Chronicle*. I spoke to her when she called to make the reservation."

Michael clenched his jaw. "What did she say her first name was?"

"You mean the whole time you were cozying up to her, you didn't ask for her first name?"

Michael scowled. "It wasn't important."

"Her name's Randi St. James."

The name struck Michael as vaguely familiar. Then suddenly he remembered why. He'd met Randi St. James two years ago at one of his book signings in New York City. While he'd autographed multiple copies of his latest cookbook—she'd bought enough for family and friends—she'd told him that she was a food critic and had enthusiastically lobbied for a Wolf's Soul to be opened in Houston.

The beautiful, alluring stranger he'd encountered tonight was *not* Randi St. James.

So who the hell was she? And what was she up to?

Noting Michael's thunderous expression, Griffin heaved a deep sigh. "Don't tell me that nice young lady isn't who she says she is."

Michael said nothing, inwardly seething. He felt like a damn fool. He was used to women employing creative tactics to get his attention, but he'd never imagined that one would go so far as to pose as a food critic. The woman was either the most aggressive fan he'd ever met, or she was seriously unbalanced for attempting such a scheme.

"Wait a minute," Griffin said. "She didn't introduce herself to you. That doesn't make any sense if she expected to receive preferential treatment. How did she know you'd find out her identity?"

"She obviously assumed *you'd* tell me," Michael muttered.

"Maybe..." Griffin was unconvinced.

Biting back an impatient oath, Michael said, "Look, I've met the real Randi St. James. Unless there are two writers by the same name reviewing restaurants for the *Houston Chronicle,* the woman is a damn liar."

He sent a dark glance toward the corridor that led to the restrooms. His mystery woman—whoever she was—had just emerged. Despite what he'd just learned about her—that she was a fraud, possibly a deranged stalker—his body still stirred at the sight of her. With her exotic beauty and a body made for sin, she was a recipe for temptation that any red-blooded male would find hard to resist. Unfortunately, that included him.

As Michael watched, she glanced around the foyer, searching for him. When their gazes connected, she gave him one of those slow, entrancing smiles that sent blood rushing straight to his groin.

Damn it all to hell. Why did she have to ruin everything by lying? They could have had such a good time together. *Incredible,* he amended, mindful of the throbbing ache between his legs.

But no matter how badly he wanted her, one thing Michael had never tolerated in women was deceitfulness. It was an automatic deal breaker for him. Always had been. Always would be.

"I think she's waiting for you," Griffin told him.

"I know," Michael murmured, holding the woman's dark gaze. "I'm driving her home."

He thought about calling her out on her lie and sending her packing. But then a better idea came to him. He'd play along with her just to see how far she was willing to go. Then, when she least suspected it, he'd spring his trap.

By the time he was through with her tonight, the woman would think twice about pulling another stunt like this.

Reese's stomach was a vicious tangle of nerves as she and Michael left downtown Atlanta and cruised onto the freeway in a sleek black Maybach. She stared out the passenger window, too preoccupied with her racing thoughts to register the passing scenery.

She couldn't believe she'd asked Michael Wolf to drive her home.

It was the most impulsive thing she'd ever done in her life. Her sister, Raina, had always teased her about being the older, wiser, sensible sister—one who was never ruled by her hormones or emotions. But *that* Reese had been nowhere to be found tonight. In her place was a woman who'd seen something she wanted and had gone after it, consequences be damned.

Boyfriend be damned.

Reese bit her lip, suffering a sharp pang of guilt at the thought of Victor. They'd only been apart for two days, and already he'd been reduced to an afterthought. She definitely hadn't been thinking about him when she'd invited Michael to keep her company over dinner. And she *definitely* hadn't been thinking about Victor when she'd asked Michael to take her home, to which he'd responded in a voice like dark velvet, "Nothing would please me more."

Reese shivered at the memory of that steamy, tantalizing exchange. She couldn't believe she'd been so bold, so reckless.

"Where are you from?"

Michael's deep voice snapped Reese out of her reverie. Startled, she turned from the window to stare blankly at him. "I'm sorry. What did you say?"

He gave her a sidelong glance. "I asked where you're from."

"Oh." She let out a breath. "Houston."

Michael nodded. "Right."

Reese thought she detected a hint of mockery in his expression. But, no, it must have been a trick of the passing streetlights.

"I've been thinking about expanding to Houston," he told her.

"Really? That'd be wonderful!" Reese grinned, unable to contain her enthusiasm. "I've been hoping you'd open a restaurant in my hometown. So have a lot of people I know."

"That's definitely good to hear. I can't take credit for the idea, though. It was pitched to me by someone I met at a book signing."

Reese nodded. "I'm no market analyst, but something tells me that Wolf's Soul would do extremely well in Houston."

"My marketing and research team seems to think so, too." He slid her a lazy smile. "Maybe you'd be the first to review the restaurant."

Reese grinned. "I'd be honored."

"I assure you, Miss St. James, the honor would be mine."

Reese flushed with pleasure. *Am I dreaming?* she wondered, not for the first time that evening. *Is any of this really happening?*

As Michael returned his attention to the road, she couldn't help admiring his handsome profile. The strong bridge of his nose, the sculpted perfection of his square jaw, the curve of those full, masculine lips she wanted so badly to kiss and taste. Her gaze drifted lower, lingering on the strong column of his throat before continuing to the hands resting on the steering wheel. They were big, broad and long fingered, the nails clipped to the quick. Reese thought about the culinary masterpieces those talented hands had produced. She could only imagine the things they could do to a woman's body. To *her* body.

At that moment Michael turned his head, meeting her gaze. Slowly he smiled, as if he'd read her mind. Her stomach fluttered.

"And to think that I almost went home after the fundraiser," he said softly. "What a shame that would have been."

"A travesty." Reese smiled. "Of course, this wasn't going to be my only visit to your restaurant. I planned to keep returning until I'd tasted everything on the menu."

Michael chuckled. "Is that right?"

"Of course." She grinned playfully. "Any food critic worth her salt knows that multiple visits to a restaurant are absolutely necessary in order to provide a fair, accurate review."

"But of course." Michael gave her a long, appraising look. "Do you enjoy what you do for a living?"

Reese's grin faded at the reminder of the hospital, and Deidra Thomas. She turned away, staring out the window. "I do enjoy my job," she said quietly. "I enjoy it very much. But if it's all the same to you, I'd rather not talk about work."

Michael said nothing.

She could feel his gaze on her, and could only speculate about what must be going through his mind. She hoped to God that she hadn't offended him. Things had been going so well between them. She didn't want to ruin the evening with depressing topics of conversation.

After a prolonged silence, Michael murmured, "You're quite an intriguing woman, Miss St. James."

Reese was about to tell him to call her by her first name when she got sidetracked by a giant image of him splashed across a billboard along the freeway. It was an advertisement for his TV show. In it Michael stood with his arms akimbo, a white chef's hat slanted low over one eye and a wickedly sexy grin curving his mouth. *Who's Afraid of the Big Bad Wolf?* the bold caption declared.

"Very clever," Reese said, laughing. "But what does the big bad wolf have to do with cooking?"

Michael chuckled. "They couldn't resist the play on my last name."

"Clearly." She stared wonderingly at him. "Do you ever get used to it?"

"What?"

"Being famous. Seeing your face plastered everywhere—on TV, on billboards, on book and magazine covers."

"It took some getting used to at first. But nowadays I don't give it much thought."

"Really?"

He glanced at her. "Fame can be fleeting. Here today, gone tomorrow. It always helps to keep things in perspective."

Reese felt her admiration for him go up another notch.

Soon they exited off I-85 and headed into Buckhead, an affluent section of Atlanta renowned for beautiful mansions, upscale shopping and fine restaurants. Reese's friend Layla lived in the historic Buckhead Forest neighborhood, an eclectic enclave of cottages, ranch houses and European stucco homes situated on wooded lots.

As Michael pulled up to a Tudor-style bungalow, the butterflies in Reese's stomach returned. *This is it,* she thought. *Once you invite him inside the house, there'll be no turning back.*

As if sensing her nervousness, Michael reached over and touched her hand, a subtle stroke that sent her pulse jumping. Their eyes met and held in the shadowy interior of the car.

"Thank you for the ride," Reese said softly.

"My pleasure. I'm glad you enjoyed your dinner tonight."

"Oh, I did. Very much." She smiled demurely. "Your company made it even better. I must have been the envy of every woman in the restaurant."

Michael smiled wryly. "*I'm* the one who was getting dirty looks from all the guys who'd been trying to work up the nerve to approach your table."

Reese laughed. "If that's true, I'm glad you beat them to it."

"Me, too," he murmured, his eyes roaming appreciatively across her face.

Reese's heart was hammering. Never before had she been so powerfully aware of a man. But this wasn't just *any* man. This was Michael Wolf, who, for the past three years, had had a starring role in her steamiest fantasies.

But this wasn't one of her fantasies. Tonight she didn't have to settle for daydreaming about Michael after watching an episode of *Howlin' Good*. Tonight she could make her dreams a reality.

So what are you waiting for?

Drawing a deep breath to summon her courage, Reese gave Michael what she hoped was her most alluring smile. "Would you like to come inside for a cup of coffee?"

His eyes glinted wickedly. They both knew what she was really offering, and it had nothing to do with the dark roast blend stashed in the kitchen cupboard.

But Michael played along. "I'd love some coffee."

Reese waited as he got out of the car and came around to her side. "Thank you," she said as he helped her out of the Maybach.

The night air was thick and sultry. Even the clouds drifted sluggishly across the moon.

"Is it always this hot during the summer?" Reese asked as they started up the walk.

Michael smiled lazily. "They don't call it Hotlanta for nothing."

"Right. Of course."

"Being from Houston," Michael drawled, "I would think you'd be used to this kind of heat."

"Oh, I am." *I'm just making inane small talk to hide the fact that I'm nervous as hell!*

"Is that your friend's car?" Michael asked as they passed a silver Lexus parked in the driveway.

"No, her car's in the garage. That's mine. I took a cab to the restaurant tonight."

"Hoping you'd meet me and talk me into giving you a ride home?" Michael teased.

Reese laughed. "Not quite."

Once they were inside the house, she set her handbag on the console table and turned on the small lamp. The soft amber glow spilled through the foyer and into the living room.

"Layla will be sorry she missed you," Reese told Michael. "She's eaten at your restaurant several times, but she's never had the pleasure of meeting you."

"How long will she be gone?" Michael asked.

"Two months."

"So we've got the place to ourselves…all night long."

Reese felt a quiver of anticipation at his words. Holding his gaze, she murmured, "All night long."

That was all the invitation Michael needed.

Before Reese could react, he dragged her into his arms, bringing her flush against his hard, powerful body. Her breath caught, and her heart rate tripled. As she stared up into his eyes, he framed her face between his hands and slanted his mouth hungrily over hers. Pleasure exploded in her veins. She wrapped her arms around his neck, melting against him with a low moan.

His lips were even softer than she'd imagined, moving sensually over hers. The taste and heat of him were unbearably arousing as he eased his tongue into her mouth slowly, deeply. She opened her mouth to him, shaking so hard she could barely stand. One of his arms went around her, holding her tightly. She kissed him back, licking into his mouth the way he was doing to her. A dark, savage sound came from his throat.

She didn't realize he was backing her up until she felt the wooden edge of the foyer table digging into her backside. Without warning an image of Victor penetrated the intoxicating haze of lust clouding her brain.

Abruptly she tore her mouth from Michael's and buried her face against his hard chest. "W-we have to stop."

He growled something that she could barely hear over the rampaging pulse in her ears.

"I'm sorry," she whispered, "but I can't do this."

"Why not?" he demanded hoarsely.

"Because…" She trailed off, words failing her. Beneath her burning cheek, she could feel his heart pounding as hard and fast as her own. She wanted him, craved him with every fiber of her being. But she couldn't have him. Despite their recent problems, she owed Victor her loyalty.

Still, it took every ounce of her willpower to pull away from Michael, and almost at once she felt bereft. "We really have to stop."

Michael stared down at her with a mixture of fascination and wry amusement. "Bravo, Miss St. James. I must admit I didn't see that coming."

Reese frowned. "What are you talking about?"

"You. Playing hard to get to make me want you even more." He shook his head slowly. "You're not the first woman who's ever tried that tactic, but you're definitely the first woman who's been successful. Congratulations."

Reese bristled. "I don't know what you're talking about. I wasn't playing hard to get."

"Weren't you?"

"Of course not."

A shadow of cynicism twisted his mouth. "Right."

Reese scowled, her temper flaring. "Look, I'm sorry if I gave you the wrong idea—"

He laughed. *"If?"*

She winced, an embarrassed flush heating her face. "Okay, fine. I asked you to drive me home tonight because I intended to seduce you. But I changed my mind. I'm sorry if I bruised your ego—"

Again his nasty bark of laughter cut her off. "My ego isn't what's bruised, sweetheart. If that kiss had lasted a second longer, you would've had me begging to make love to you. Trust me, that had *nothing* to do with my ego."

Her face grew hotter. "Look, the kiss was a mistake."

His jaw hardened. "You're damn right it was, Miss St. James, or whatever the hell your real name is."

"What's that supposed to mean?" Reese demanded, frowning in confusion. "That *is* my real name."

"Right," Michael said mockingly. "I suppose you're also going to tell me that you're a food critic."

"*What?* Why on earth would I tell you something like that?"

"Oh, I don't know. Maybe because you're delusional. Or maybe because you're a damn liar."

Stunned, Reese gaped at him, feeling as though she'd been transported to some alternate universe where all of the inhabitants spoke in strange riddles. What Michael was accusing her of made no sense whatsoever.

Striving for composure, she said evenly, "Look, there must be some misunderstanding. I never claimed to be a food critic—"

"My maître d' seems to think otherwise."

"Then he's mistaken!"

"Is he?" Michael challenged, his eyes narrowing on hers. "So what about that line you fed me in the car? The one about 'any food critic worth her salt' knowing that multiple visits to a restaurant are necessary to write fair reviews. Weren't you implying that you're a food critic?"

"No! I was just flirting with you!" Struck by a sudden realization, Reese eyed him incredulously. "Wait a minute. Are you suggesting that I pretended to be a restaurant critic just to get your attention?"

"I think that's obvious."

"No, it's *ridiculous*. You must be out of your damn mind!"

"Said the pot to the kettle."

Reese glared at him. "If you think I'm such a nutcase, why did you agree to drive me home? What does that say about *you*?"

His expression hardened. "I plead temporary insanity. Trust me, it won't happen again."

Without another word, he spun on his heel and stalked out the front door.

Reese charged after him, her chest heaving with fury. No way was she letting him have the last word!

"I know this may be hard for you to accept, you arrogant son of a bitch, but you're *not* God's gift to women. Believe it or not, there *are* a few of us who are perfectly capable of resisting your charms."

Pausing at his car door, Michael glared back at her, his eyes hard and glittering in the night.

Reese wasn't finished. "I'm so glad I found out what an asshole you are before I wasted another second of my time watching your damn show. And you wanna know something else? I've always liked Bobby Flay better, anyway!"

Before Michael could respond, she slammed the door hard enough to give the neighbors something to talk about.

As far as she was concerned, being fodder for gossip was a small price to pay for the sweet satisfaction of having the last word with Michael. After the abominable way he'd treated her tonight, she'd take whatever victory she could get.

Chapter 3

Michael was still in a foul mood when he woke up the next morning at his father's house, where he often spent the night to keep Sterling Wolf company.

To burn off steam, Michael threw on some sweats and went for a run through the idyllic Stone Mountain neighborhood.

He couldn't get the woman from last night out of his mind. Every time he replayed the encounter in his mind, he grew more angry and disgusted with himself. But what bothered him more than anything was that he couldn't shake the nagging suspicion that he'd been wrong about the woman. Maybe she'd been telling the truth after all. Maybe her last name really *was* St. James, and somehow Griffin had gotten her confused with the Houston food critic.

Michael's cell phone rang as he returned to the silent house. He dug it out of his pocket and checked the caller ID. It was Drew Corbett, the executive producer of his cooking show.

"Hey, Mike," Drew greeted him, brisk and annoyingly upbeat even at such an early hour. "How was the whirlwind book tour?"

"Great," Michael muttered, heading toward the kitchen to start breakfast before his father woke up. "I'm already looking forward to the next trip."

"Of course. We all know how much you love being on the road." Drew paused. "Not!"

Michael grinned wryly. One of the drawbacks to being a celebrity chef was that he sometimes felt like he did more performing than cooking. Although he understood that touring and promoting his brand were vital to his success, he often wished he could leave that stuff to someone else so he could focus on what he enjoyed most: cooking. He loved being a chef. He loved rising to the challenge of creating unique, delicious meals that would satisfy even the most finicky eaters. He loved the pressure-cooker intensity of the kitchen. He loved taking a new cook under his wing, and he thrived on the camaraderie he shared with his staff. Hell, he didn't even mind the long hours. Being a chef was physically, mentally and emotionally demanding.

And he wouldn't trade it for the world.

After taking a swig of bottled water, he asked, "What's up, Drew? You calling to tell me the meeting's been re-scheduled?"

"Not at all. Actually, I just wanted to make sure you hadn't forgotten about it. I figured you'd be sleeping off some jet lag this morning, so I decided not to call you too early."

"Thanks," Michael mumbled.

"Everyone at the studio is really excited about the new season of *Howlin' Good*," Drew said. "I think our viewers are gonna get a real kick out of the apprentice series. As you might imagine, we were inundated with contest entries from all over the country. We've finally gone through all of them and selected our ten finalists."

"That's good."

"Our test kitchen favorite was a curry chicken soufflé submitted by a woman from Houston," Drew continued. "I think even *you'd* be impressed with the recipe, that's how good it was."

"Is that right? And you say she's from Houston?"

"Yeah."

"What's her name?"

"Hang on a sec." The noise of rustling papers could be heard in the background. After another moment Drew came back on the line. "Here's the file. Her name's Reese St. James."

Michael blinked. "Come again?"

"It's Reese St. James." Drew sounded puzzled. "Is there a problem?"

"No." A grim smile curved Michael's mouth. "It's just… ironic."

"What's ironic?"

"I met a woman last night who claimed her last name was St. James."

"Claimed?"

"Long story. Anyway, tell me more about this finalist."

"According to her entry form, she's an ob-gyn at Methodist Hospital in Houston. She enjoys cooking as a stress reliever. She wrote that if she weren't a doctor, she'd probably be a food critic."

Michael went still. Could Reese St. James be the same woman he'd met last night? What were the odds?

"I already called to notify her that she finaled in the contest," Drew said.

"You spoke to her?"

"No, I left a message on her voice mail yesterday. I was going to try her again this morning. She's the only finalist I haven't spoken to, and I want to make sure she's available to fly here for the auditions on Friday."

Michael frowned as a new thought occurred to him. If Reese St. James was the woman he'd met last night, had she known that she was a finalist in his contest when she showed up at the restaurant last night? If so, why hadn't she mentioned it to him? Had she planned to seduce him in the hopes that he'd choose her to be his apprentice?

Only one way to find out.

"Why don't you let me call her back?" he suggested.

"You?" Drew asked in surprise.

"Sure. Why not? After the way you raved about the recipe she submitted, I have to admit I'm a little curious about her. She could be the one."

"Maybe," Drew hedged. "But none of the other finalists received a personal phone call from you. It might look fishy, like we're playing favorites."

"Why don't you let me worry about that?" Michael said smoothly. "What's her number?"

Sleep hadn't diminished Reese's anger.

Not that she'd actually gotten much sleep.

She'd tossed and turned throughout the night, reliving every embarrassing second of her confrontation with Michael Wolf. She couldn't believe he'd accused her of impersonating a food critic in order to lure him into bed. Of all the damn nerve!

And to think that she'd spent the past three years admiring the man and fantasizing about him. She should have known better. She was thirty-four years old, too damn old to have idolized—and idealized—a perfect stranger. Michael Wolf was a celebrity chef, a TV personality who entertained people for a living. It shouldn't have shocked her to discover that the man behind the charming persona was arrogant, cruel and conniving. Yet she *was* shocked. And humiliated.

While *she'd* been thinking what a great guy he was, *he'd* been secretly laying a trap for her, waiting for the perfect opportunity to make a fool out of her.

Bastard, Reese thought with renewed anger. If she never saw Michael Wolf again, it'd be too soon.

Turning her head on the pillow, she leveled a bleary-eyed glare at the bedside clock. It was just after seven. Bars of sunlight slanted through the shutters that covered the bedroom windows. Reese couldn't have gotten more than two hours of sleep last night, but she was too agitated to stay in bed any longer. She might as well take a shower and go about her business. Michael Wolf had already cost her one sleepless night. She'd be damned if she let him ruin her entire day.

Remembering that she'd turned off her cell phone at the restaurant last night, Reese reached inside her handbag on the floor. When her searching fingers encountered the smooth surface of a hardcover book, she felt a fresh burst of anger. It was Michael's cookbook, which she'd taken to dinner hoping to get his autograph.

Scowling, Reese yanked the book out of her purse and hurled it across the room. It hit the wall with a loud, satisfying thud and slid to the floor. Making a mental note to toss it into the fireplace the first chance she got, she pulled out her cell phone and pressed the button to retrieve her voice mail messages.

As expected, the first one was from Victor. "Hi. It's me. I guess you're out having dinner right now. Alone, I hope."

Reese bit her bottom lip, guilt gnawing at her conscience as he continued. "Look, I know I agreed to give you time to settle in before I called, but…I miss you. I wish you'd reconsider staying in Atlanta for the whole summer. It's not fair to either one of us. I—" Catching himself, he broke off and blew out a deep breath. "I know I promised not to badger you about this. Just…give me a call as soon as you can."

As the message ended, Reese fell back against her pillows and groaned. Why was Victor making this so difficult? Why couldn't he give her the breathing room she so desperately needed? Didn't he understand that this separation period could ultimately *help* their relationship?

The next message rolled on. "Hello, Dr. St. James. This is Drew Corbett, executive producer of *Howlin' Good with Michael Wolf.* I was calling to congratulate you on being a finalist in our apprentice contest. I'd like to invite you to Atlanta to audition for the show this Friday. Please call me as soon as possible to discuss the arrangements."

As he rattled off his phone number, Reese sat up slowly, her eyes wide with shock. Was someone playing a prank on her? Was Ashton Kutcher waiting to jump out of her closet to smugly announce that she'd just been "punk'd"?

Six months ago, Reese had been watching *Howlin' Good* when Michael Wolf announced to viewers that he was launching a nationwide search for an apprentice to appear on his show that fall. On a whim Reese had entered the contest, never expecting anything to come of it. Between work, Victor and helping to plan her sister's wedding, she'd forgotten all about the contest. And now she learned that she was a finalist?

"Un-freaking-believable," she whispered.

If she'd received the news twenty-four hours ago, she would have been positively ecstatic. But after last night's disastrous encounter with Michael Wolf, Reese wanted absolutely nothing to do with the despicable man.

What a difference a night makes.

Since she had no intention of auditioning for the show, she decided she'd better return the producer's call so he could find another sucker to replace her.

She'd just jotted down the man's number when her cell phone rang.

She checked the caller ID and frowned. It was an unfamiliar number with a local area code. The only person Reese knew from Atlanta was Layla Chase, and she was halfway around the world in Somalia.

Realizing that the caller might be the television producer, Reese answered the phone. "Hello?"

"Miss St. James?" a deep, masculine voice rumbled into her ear.

Her traitorous heart knocked against her ribs. That voice. She'd recognize it *anywhere*. "Yes?"

"This is Michael Wolf."

Reese moistened her dry lips. "What do you want?" she asked curtly.

"It seems that I owe you an apology."

Reese sat up straighter in bed. It was the *last* thing she'd expected to hear from Michael. Hell, she hadn't expected to hear from him at all!

"I'm listening," she said coolly.

"Last night I accused you of lying about your identity, and I was wrong. So I'm calling to apologize."

Reese was silent, caught off guard by the sincerity in his voice. She knew she should accept his apology and leave it at that, but she just couldn't let him off the hook that easily. Not after the way he'd humiliated her.

"What possessed you to accuse me of something so outrageous?"

"It was a misunderstanding," Michael said evenly. "My maître d' must have gotten you confused with a food critic who has a similar name. Ever heard of Randi St. James?"

"No."

"Apparently she also had dinner reservations. My guess is that my maître d' got your names and dates mixed up. When the restaurant opens at ten, I'll call and have someone check the reservation database for me. But I'm pretty sure that's what happened."

"In the future," Reese said drily, "you should probably get your facts straight before you go around maligning innocent people. Especially when those people are paying customers."

"Point taken." There was a note of wry amusement in his voice. "I understand congratulations are in order. You're a finalist in my apprentice contest."

"Imagine that," Reese said with as much enthusiasm as if he'd told her it was going to rain.

"My producer tells me he called you yesterday."

"Yes, he did. My cell phone was turned off, so I just received his message this morning." She paused, then added sarcastically, "Just in case you think I had an ulterior motive for not telling you last night that I was a finalist."

When Michael said nothing, Reese frowned.

"Wait a minute," she said suspiciously. "You didn't actually *think* that, did you?"

He hesitated. "The thought may have crossed my mind."

"I don't believe you!" Reese burst out, indignation launching her from the bed. "Just how conceited *are* you?"

He made an impatient sound. "I'm not—"

"Yes, you are! Only a conceited jerk would concoct outrageous scenarios in which women are so desperate to be with him that they resort to lying and impersonating others just to have him." She shook her head in disgust. "Congratulations, Mr. Wolf. In one fell swoop, you've gone from being my favorite chef to the most arrogant, overbearing man I've ever met."

"I thought Bobby Flay was your favorite chef," Michael snidely reminded her.

"He is now!"

"Good. Then why don't you go and audition for *his* show? Oh, wait, that's right. You entered a contest to become *my* apprentice."

"I plead temporary insanity," Reese jeered. "Trust me, it won't happen again."

"I'm so glad you feel that way, Miss St. James—"

"That's *Doctor* to you," Reese snarled, though she'd never been hung up on titles.

"Fine. As I was saying, *Dr.* St. James," Michael replied, bitingly mocking, "I'm glad you realize that you made a mistake by entering the contest. Showing up for the audition would have been a huge waste of your time and mine. It wouldn't have worked out between us."

"That's probably the understatement of the year!"

"Good," Michael said tersely. "I'll let my producer know that you've decided to withdraw from the competition. Goodbye, Dr. St. James. Have a nice life."

"Wait a minute," Reese snapped. "Where do you get off putting words in my mouth? I never said anything about withdrawing from the competition."

"What the hell are you talking about?" Michael growled. "You just told me that entering the contest was a mistake."

"It was! But that doesn't mean I'm about to cavalierly walk

away from a chance to win one hundred thousand dollars." She paused, then couldn't resist adding spitefully, "You didn't think I was only interested in being your lowly apprentice, did you?"

"I don't really give a damn. There's not a chance in hell you're winning that contest."

"Says who?" Reese challenged.

"*I* say."

"Is that so? Well, it's my understanding that the apprentice will be chosen based on who has the strongest audition."

"And who do you think has the final say on that? Trust me, if I don't think I can work with you, it's a no-go. So do yourself a favor and stay home on Friday."

"I don't think so. I finaled in that contest fair and square. You have no right—"

"I have every right. It's my show, my contest, my rules."

"Yeah? We'll see about that."

Reese hung up on him, snatched up the prescription pad where she'd written down the producer's contact information and quickly punched in the number.

When she got Drew Corbett on the phone, she said sweetly, "Good morning, Mr. Corbett. This is Reese St. James."

"Hello! Thanks for returning my call. First things first. Can you make it to Atlanta for Friday's audition? I have my assistant on standby to book your flight."

"Oh, that won't be necessary," Reese said smoothly. "As luck would have it, I'm already in town."

Chapter 4

"Eight down, two to go."

Reese smiled at the perky blonde seated next to her in the television studio's green room. The woman had been chattering nonstop ever since she and Reese, along with eight other apprentice hopefuls, had been herded into the room to await their turn to audition.

"I'm so nervous," the blonde confided. "I *love* Michael Wolf. I can't wait to meet him."

Reese merely smiled. It wasn't that long ago she'd felt the same way. Now she knew better. The only reason she'd decided to show up for today's audition was to spite Michael. She had no interest in sharing a stage with him or winning any money. Her game plan was simple: knock the judges' socks off. If she won the competition, she'd politely decline the apprenticeship by citing "irreconcilable differences" with Michael, which would put him in the awkward position of having to explain himself to his colleagues.

Revenge is a dish best served cold, Reese thought with wicked satisfaction.

When it was her turn, she followed the production assistant down a long, narrow corridor and through an open doorway that brought them to the set of *Howlin' Good*.

Despite her newfound loathing for Michael Wolf, Reese couldn't help feeling a rush of excitement as she started down the aisle toward the kitchen at center stage. With its gleaming mahogany cabinets, granite countertops and modern stainless steel appliances, the set of *Howlin' Good* had become as familiar to her as her own kitchen. To be here in person was surreal.

Her fascinated gaze took in a kaleidoscope of cameras, lights, monitors and microphones. A network of lights hung from the ceiling, facing in various directions and at different angles. There were several technicians milling around, checking lighting, adjusting equipment and giving instructions to one another. A small group of people stood chatting around a table that had been erected in front of the stage—the judges, Reese realized when she spied another popular chef whose cable show she often watched.

For the first time since her arrival at the studio two hours ago, she began to feel nervous.

The feeling only intensified when she glanced around and saw Michael emerge from a doorway to the right of the stage. He was followed by his executive producer, whom Reese had met that morning, and a man wearing a headset and carrying a clipboard.

As Reese watched Michael stride purposefully toward the stage, she wondered how anyone could look so mouthwateringly good in a simple black T-shirt and jeans. But the shirt clung enticingly to his broad, muscular chest, and the jeans rode wickedly low on his hips.

As if sensing her hungry appraisal, Michael turned his head, his dark eyes scanning the crowded set before homing in on hers. Reese's breath caught. Her pulse thudded as his gaze swept over her, taking in her white ruffle blouse and linen slacks before easing back up to her face. Though his expression didn't change, there was no mistaking the subtle challenge that glinted in his eyes.

Reese lifted her chin defiantly, answering with her own silent message: *Bring it on!*

A smile played at the corners of his lips before he glanced away to finish conferring with his producer.

"You're on in three minutes." The production assistant led Reese onto the stage, where a cameraman clipped a tiny microphone to her lapel. "For the audition, you're going to assist Michael with preparing a basic recipe. As I told the other contestants, the judges are more interested in your stage presence and the way you interact with Michael than your culinary skills. So just relax and be yourself."

"Good advice," Reese murmured, trying not to notice that dozens of strangers were watching and critiquing her every move. She was relieved that she didn't have to audition before a live studio audience.

Michael awaited her at the large center island that was the focal point of the kitchen. It featured a restaurant-style electric cooktop and enough counter space for him to spread out his ingredients and display his culinary masterpieces at the end of each episode.

As Reese took her place beside him, he slanted her a faintly mocking glance. "Think you can keep up?"

She smiled sweetly at him. "I was just about to ask you the same thing."

Before he could respond, the director began his countdown. "Five, four, three, two—"

On cue Michael flashed his trademark grin into the camera—the slow, wicked grin that melted women the world over and kept their eyes glued to their television sets. "Today we'll be whipping up a classic Southern favorite—shrimp and grits. As any true Southerner knows, eating grits is a way of life, and breakfast without 'em is downright sacrilegious, as my father likes to say. But grits aren't just for breakfast anymore, and today we're gonna show you why. But first I'd like to introduce you to the lovely Reese St. James, who'll be assisting me in the kitchen today."

Reese smiled and waved as the people gathered around the set applauded loudly in an effort to simulate a live audience.

"Reese hails from the Lone Star state," Michael said, smiling so easily at her no one would have believed they were enemies. "Houston, right?"

"That's right," Reese said cheerfully. "It's a pleasure to be here with you, Michael. Feel free to put me right to work."

Michael grinned at the onlookers. "Doesn't waste any time, does she?" he drawled with a suggestive wink that earned him a round of hearty laughter.

Not to be outdone, Reese picked up a piece of chilled shrimp from a bowl on the counter. "So what're we working with today, shrimp? Er, I mean *chef.*"

More laughter filled the room.

"That's right, Reese," Michael said, plucking the shrimp out of her fingers and dropping it into the bowl. "Today we're working with shrimp. I've got some big, fat, juicy—"

Reese fanned herself with her hand, drawing another burst of raucous laughter. Someone even whistled.

Shaking his head, Michael muttered under his breath, "Good help is so hard to find," which elicited some sympathetic chuckles.

"What do you want me to do, Michael?" Reese asked sweetly.

He looked her up and down slowly, then raised his eyes heavenward. "Lord, why do you tempt me so?"

More chortles and catcalls ensued.

When the noise had subsided, Michael said to Reese, "Why don't you stir those grits on the stove?" As Reese moved to comply, he explained to the audience, "Most folks use instant grits, and that's fine if you're pressed for time. But I'm a purist who believes that the best grits are stone-ground and cooked slowly in butter and cream for at least two hours."

"Two hours?" Reese echoed in surprise.

"Absolutely." He met her gaze, his voice dipping low. "The slower, the better."

Reese's belly flip-flopped as the onlookers reacted with wolf whistles. This time she really *did* need to fan herself.

"So while your grits are simmering on the stove," Michael continued, dragging his gaze from hers, "you need to spice up your shrimp. Being a Southern boy, I like mine really spicy. So that means plenty of Cajun seasoning, as well as Italian seasoning, paprika, salt and pepper. You're gonna sprinkle the combined spices over the shrimp until they're good and coated. And then you're ready to sauté them bad boys."

As he pulled out a large pan and joined Reese at the stove, he said gruffly, "Keep stirring, woman. I don't want my grits sticking to the bottom and burning."

Reese gave a mock salute. "Yes, sir." Under her breath she muttered, "You can kiss *my* grits."

As laughter erupted around the set, Michael leaned close to her, his hand cupped to his ear. "I didn't hear that. Did you say something?"

Reese batted her lashes innocently. "I said, 'You're the boss.'"

His mouth twitched. "Yeah, I thought so." Turning on the burner next to hers, he said, "In a large pan, you're gonna add two tablespoons of olive oil and minced garlic. Heat it up and stir for about thirty seconds, then throw in your seasoned shrimp—"

"Throw?" Reese interrupted skeptically. "Are you sure you should be telling viewers to throw anything into a skillet of hot oil?"

When Michael just stared at her, she said grimly, "I'm a doctor. I've seen more than enough third-degree burns caused by household cooking accidents. Might I suggest you find another verb?"

He gaped at her a moment longer, then nodded tightly. "All right," he agreed, addressing the camera. "You're gonna *ease* the shrimp into the pan—"

"Oh, much better. I like *ease*."

Michael looked at Reese as if he wanted to clobber her over the head with the pan. "Anything else?" he inquired through clenched teeth.

She grinned sheepishly. "Nope. I'm good." The audience chortled as she hunched over the pot of grits and stirred with renewed vigor.

"As I was saying," Michael continued with exaggerated patience, "after you add the shrimp, sauté them for about three minutes—just until they're tender. You don't wanna overcook them. When they're done, remove them from the pan and set 'em aside in a bowl."

"But *not* in the same bowl that had the raw shrimp, right?" Reese interjected. At his blank look, she hastened to clarify herself. "I mean, I know seafood doesn't warrant the same cross-contamination concerns as poultry, but just to be on the safe side…"

"Of course," Michael said with a steely smile for the camera. "You're going to place the cooked shrimp in a *different* bowl. Just like I did."

"Wonderful. Mmm, those look delicious," Reese breathed, eyeing the mound of sautéed shrimp. "Can I have—"

"No," Michael snapped, moving the bowl out of her reach. The audience chuckled while Reese pretended to pout.

Deliberately ignoring her, Michael continued, "Now comes the roux, which is basically a cooked mixture of flour and fat that's used to thicken many Cajun dishes. So here's what you're gonna do, folks." He explained the next few steps, demonstrating as he went along. "After you've cooked the roux, add a teaspoon of Worcestershire sauce and hot sauce. I usually make my own hot sauce, but if you're looking for a shortcut, a good brand I recommend is Texas Pete—"

"Hey, I think I know him!" Reese piped up brightly.

This set off a new wave of laughter.

Michael shook his head at the ceiling, but his lips were quirking, as if he wanted to smile but wouldn't give her the satisfaction. It didn't matter, though. Reese knew he was having as much fun as she was, even if he'd sooner eat stewed lizard guts than admit it.

Grinning, she removed the grits from the burner. "What're you gonna do with those?" she asked, pointing to another bowl filled with neat cubes of sautéed country ham.

"Watch and learn."

Michael heaped a few spoonfuls of grits onto a plate and topped it with several sizzling pieces of shrimp. Next he poured a liberal amount of the roux sauce over the shrimp, added a sprinkling of ham, then presented the finished dish with a dramatic, *"Booyah!"*

Reese joined in the vigorous applause that swept around the room. *"Now* may I have a taste?" she entreated him. "Pretty please?"

Michael grinned lazily. "Sure. Why not?"

He scooped up a forkful of shrimp and grits and brought it to her mouth. Reese opened her mouth automatically for him. As her lips closed around the fork, his gaze darkened. She let out a soft groan. "Mmmm. That is *sooo* good."

Watching her intently, Michael sampled a bite, licking their shared fork in a way that made Reese's nipples harden and her pulse accelerate.

Their gazes held for a long, charged moment.

"Cut!" the director called out suddenly. In a voice laced with amusement, he added, "And would someone please bring me a glass of cold water? It's hot in here!"

An hour later, Drew Corbett was still raving about Reese St. James's audition performance. And he wasn't the only one. From the production assistant to the casting director, the consensus around the studio was that Reese should, and *would* be, Michael's new apprentice.

He seemed to be the only one who thought otherwise.

"She was brilliant," Drew declared to Michael and the four contest judges who'd gathered in the conference room to compare notes on the auditions. "She was totally at ease in front of the camera, she seemed comfortable in the kitchen *and* she had great comedic timing. The way she played comic ingenue to Mike's 'straight man' reminded me of something you'd see on *I Love Lucy*. And let's face it, folks. She's not exactly hard on the eyes. The camera loves her."

There were hearty murmurs of agreement around the table.

Paige Somers, a leggy brunette who worked as a senior editor at *Food & Wine* magazine in New York, raved, "Let me just add that I absolutely *loved* the sexual chemistry between Reese and Michael."

"Chemistry?" echoed a petite, pretty black woman named Lexi Austin. "That was a five-alarm fire!"

Everyone laughed.

"I've judged a lot of cooking competitions in my career," Paige continued with a broad grin, "but I have *never* seen anything hotter than when Michael fed Reese from his fork, then took a bite himself. Whew!" she exclaimed, fanning her face. "I think we all wanted to jump in a cold pool after that!"

Lexi snorted. "Speak for yourself. I wanted to jump *Michael!*"

More uproarious laughter filled the room. Even Michael, who'd been heretofore silent, couldn't suppress a low chuckle.

Drew glanced around the table, a huge, satisfied grin on his face. "These are the types of conversations women will be having at water coolers, on park benches and over coffee with their friends once Reese St. James makes her debut on the show. The chemistry between her and Michael is pure ratings gold. Their sharp repartee, the crackling sexual tension—our viewers are gonna eat it up."

"I agree," Paige said vigorously, and the others nodded.

"We all seem to be on the same page," Lexi noted, "but we haven't heard what the star of the show thinks."

Michael smiled as five pairs of eyes swung in his direction. He'd been sprawled in a chair at the head of the table, eyes hooded, arms folded behind his head, long legs stretched out in front of him. Anyone observing his lazy posture might have assumed he'd tuned out the discussion long ago. But Michael—as everyone who worked with him knew—never missed a thing.

Still, it didn't surprise him that Lexi had been the first to draw attention to his silence. She knew him better than anyone else in the room, as they'd been friends for over twenty years. They'd met as freshmen in college; Michael had attended Morehouse while Lexi was a student at Spelman. They'd hit it off right away, bonding over their mutual love for good food and cooking. When they graduated, Lexi had followed her true passion and gone to a French culinary school in New York while Michael went to work for a top engineering firm—a move Lexi still teased him about to this day. As a master chef instructor at a culinary institute in Atlanta, she was highly respected in the world of culinary arts. Michael considered her more than a friend; she was also a trusted advisor.

"You wanna know what I think?" he drawled, straightening slowly in the chair. "I think that *Howlin' Good* is a family-friendly show, one that stay-at-home moms can watch with their young children without having to worry about being bombarded with sexual innuendo. If we want to keep it that way—and keep the show off the FCC's hit list—we'd better choose someone other than Reese St. James to be the apprentice."

A ripple of laughter went around the table.

"Michael Sterling Wolf," Lexi said, feigning a shocked tone. "Are you suggesting that you wouldn't be able to control yourself around Reese?"

Michael grinned sheepishly, rubbing his jaw. "It'd be damn hard, I can tell you that."

He'd had a hard enough time keeping his hands off Reese during the short time they'd been on stage together. Her coquettish smiles had been disarming enough, but when she parted those lush lips, took his fork slowly into her mouth and moaned, he'd nearly lost his mind. He'd wanted to make love to her right then and there, spectators be damned.

"Apart from the fact that you don't trust yourself not to jump Reese's bones," Paige said, "what other objections do you have to working with her?"

For a moment Michael considered coming clean about everything that had transpired between him and Reese. But he quickly changed his mind. It was bad enough that he'd been forced to eat crow and apologize to her. If his colleagues ever found out what an ass he'd made of himself, he'd never live it down.

And something told him that was exactly what Reese wanted. He didn't believe for one second that she was interested in the prize money, or even fifteen minutes of fame. She'd come to the audition for one reason and one reason only: to get back at him.

So far, her plan was working brilliantly. She had everyone eating out of the palm of her hand, ensuring that Michael would be the bad guy if he refused to work with her. But refuse he must.

"Look, I'm not disagreeing that she gave a great performance. She did. I just think we should keep our options open."

Paige's eyebrows shot up. "Who else came close to being as good as Reese?"

Michael racked his brain trying to recall the other contestants' faces, but most of them were a blur. As much as he hated to admit it, the only one who'd stood out was Reese.

"You have to admit that the stars seem to be aligned in her favor," Drew said, pressing his advantage. "First the recipe she submitted was our test kitchen favorite. Then she just happened to be in Atlanta when we notified her. As it turns out she'll be here on sabbatical for the next two months, which means she'll be available for taping the apprentice episodes and attending any publicity events we ask of her. And if that's still not enough proof that she's the right woman for the job, she just gave an audition performance that was clearly head and shoulders above the rest." He cast an impatient glance around the table. "Quite honestly, I'm surprised we're even debating this."

"Well," Lexi argued diplomatically, "with all due respect, boss man, it *is* Michael's show. And since he's the one who's going to be working closely with this apprentice for the next few weeks, it's only right that he get the final say on who it will be."

Michael smiled at his old friend. *Finally! A voice of reason.* "Thank you, Lexi."

"That said," she added, dark eyes twinkling, "I think you'd be out of your mind not to pick Reese St. James."

Everyone laughed.

Everyone but Michael. Leaning back in his chair, he blew out a deep, frustrated breath.

"Well?" Drew prompted, eyeing him expectantly. "What's the verdict? Is the doctor in?"

Michael's jaw tightened. "Yeah," he muttered darkly, "but if we end up getting hate mail from scandalized stay-at-home moms, don't say I didn't warn you."

Chapter 5

Reese was in a daze.

She'd just gotten off the phone with Drew Corbett, who'd called to tell her that she'd won the apprentice competition. He'd praised her audition performance as "captivating" and "brilliant." Reese had been floored, and undeniably flattered. Perhaps that would explain why, when she opened her mouth to politely decline the offer—as she'd planned—what came out instead was, "Thank you so much for this incredible opportunity. I look forward to working with you!"

After the call ended, she'd stared incredulously at the phone in her hand. She couldn't believe how easily she'd abandoned her plan to get even with Michael. What on earth had gotten into her?

Who are you kidding? her conscience mocked. *You never had any intention of turning down the opportunity to work with Michael Wolf. Who in their right mind would?*

Despite everything Reese had told herself, and despite the fact that she'd spent the past three days calling him everything but a child of God, she still wanted Michael. He'd awakened something deep inside her. Something wanton, delicious, intoxicating.

Something dangerously irresistible.

She couldn't have stayed away from him if her life depended on it.

Her cell phone jangled suddenly, jerking her out of her trance. When she saw Victor's number, her face heated with shame, as though he'd intercepted her traitorous thoughts from hundreds of miles away. She considered ignoring the call, but she knew she couldn't avoid him forever.

Blowing out a deep breath that ruffled her long bangs, she answered the phone. "Hello, there."

"Reese? Thank God you picked up." Victor sounded both relieved and exasperated. "I was just about to call your sister to see if we needed to file a missing person's report with the police."

"Don't be so melodramatic," Reese said drily. "Besides, Raina wouldn't have appreciated being awakened early in the morning."

"What do you mean?"

"She and Warrick are attending that conference in Italy, remember?"

"Oh, that's right. I forgot."

Reese had nearly forgotten herself. She'd been dying to call her sister and tell her everything that had happened in the past four days. In fact, on the night she'd met Michael, she'd excused herself after dinner and made a beeline for the restroom just to call Raina. She'd dialed her sister's number before she remembered that Raina was out of the country with her husband, Warrick. Since returning from their honeymoon three months ago, the newlyweds had been inseparable, and while this recent trip was for business, Reese had no doubt that they'd spend as much time *in* bed as out of it.

"We should have gone with them after all," Victor said wistfully. "I could have shown you guys around Venice and taken you to some of the best places in the world to eat. We could have had a wonderful time together." He sighed. "If only you and I weren't such workaholics."

Reese refrained from pointing out to him that *he* was the one who'd cited their busy schedules when Raina approached them with the idea of accompanying her and Warrick on their overseas business trip. Reese had been willing to take time off from work for a romantic excursion to Italy, but Victor had refused.

His remark was just another example of his selective memory. Apparently he'd also chosen to forget that he'd promised to give Reese space. Calling her every day wasn't what she'd had in mind when she'd asked for a breather.

"I've left you several messages," he told her. "Did you get them?"

"Yes. I haven't had a chance to call you back." *You haven't given me a chance,* Reese added silently.

"So what have you been doing with yourself? Done any sightseeing?"

"A little." Inside the kitchen, Reese walked to the refrigerator and removed a plate of thawed veal cutlets she'd seasoned earlier to make veal parmigiana for dinner. She'd made a pact with herself not to eat out more than twice a week, although it was tempting with so many great restaurants to choose from.

"Why are you being so vague?" Victor complained. "I'm not interrogating you. I just want to know what you've been up to."

Reese gave him a quick rundown of her week. Other than to mention having dinner at Wolf's Soul, she didn't elaborate on her encounters with Michael Wolf, or the apprenticeship. She didn't feel like dealing with Victor's jealousy.

"How long are you going to keep running away, Reese?" *Here we go.* "Don't start."

"Damn it, Reese, can't you see how crazy this is, how irrational you're behaving? If I skipped town every time *I* lost a patient—"

Anger slashed through her. "Don't *even* go there."

Victor sighed. "Reese—"

"No," she snapped, her voice trembling with leashed anger. "I don't want to have this conversation with you. You made your feelings perfectly clear before I left. There's nothing more to discuss."

"*Merda!* Would you just listen to me?"

"I've heard enough!" she shouted. "God, I can't believe you'd be callous enough to throw Deidra Thomas's death in my face like that! The most awful day of my life was the day I had to look her husband in the eye and tell him he had to raise their three young children alone. I will *never* forget—" Her voice broke, and she blinked back tears.

"Reese—" Victor began.

"I've been trying my damnedest not to think about what that poor man and his family must be going through. It hasn't been easy, but I'm trying." She swallowed a hard knot of emotion. "Maybe I'm not as strong as you are, Victor. Maybe you would have handled Deidra's death better. But *I* needed to get away for a while and clear my head, and I'm not going to apologize for that."

"I never asked you to," Victor said defensively.

"Could've fooled me," Reese shot back.

He heaved a breath. "Let's not argue anymore, *cara mia.* Please?"

There was a time Reese would have melted at the endearment. Now she just felt annoyed, as if he were trying to manipulate her by speaking Italian. It wouldn't be the first time.

She sighed. "Look, I should go. I want to finish making dinner so I can catch a movie later."

"Alone?"

"Yes," she bit off. *"Alone."*

"Will you call me tomorrow?"

"No."

"Can I call you?"

"I'd rather you didn't." When he started to protest, she

said firmly, "Give me at least a week, Victor. *One* week. I'm serious."

He sighed harshly in her ear. "If that's what you really want—"

"It is."

"Fine. Have it your way."

"Thank you. Good night."

Reese hung up and dropped her cell phone onto the countertop with a loud clatter. She could feel the onset of a headache behind her eyelids, and as she surveyed the veal cutlets she'd removed from the refrigerator, she realized she'd lost her appetite.

Damn you, Victor, she thought rancorously.

Abandoning her plans to make dinner, she strode to the butler's pantry and snagged a bottle of cabernet sauvignon from the wine rack. She poured herself a glass and headed into the living room. As she sank into a comfy armchair, her gaze landed on Michael's *Howlin' Good* cookbook on the fireplace mantel, where she'd placed it so she wouldn't forget to burn it.

That was three days ago. The rage she'd felt toward Michael had lessened considerably since then. Truth be told, she was angrier with Victor at the moment than Michael. So angry, in fact, that she was beginning to think that their relationship couldn't be saved. It had been on life support for a long time.

Maybe it was time to finally pull the plug.

Chapter 6

"Uncle Mike! Uncle Mike!"

Michael had just stepped out of his car when two miniature tornadoes, in the form of his three-year-old nephews, came hurtling down the driveway toward him. By the time he closed the car door, the twins had launched themselves at his legs. Laughing, Michael reached down and scooped them into his arms, planting an affectionate kiss on top of each boy's head.

"Hey, pups," he greeted them. "How was Disney World?"

"Fun!" Matthew and Malcolm Wolf chorused, their identical faces lit up with wide, dimpled smiles. "You shoulda come with us!"

Michael chuckled, watching as his brother, Marcus, sauntered toward him. "I wish I could have, but I had to work. Maybe next time."

"You promise?" entreated Matthew, who'd already established himself as the more demanding twin.

Coming to Michael's rescue, Marcus said chidingly, "Little

boy, your mother and I need to catch our breath before we even *think* about taking any more trips to Orlando."

Michael grinned at his brother. "Ran you ragged, didn't they?"

Marcus chuckled. "Let's just say I've never felt so old in my life."

"That's because you *are* old."

"Hey, look who's talking!"

Though almost six years apart, Michael and Marcus had often been described as dead ringers of each other. Like Michael, Marcus was tall, broad-shouldered and long-legged, with smooth mahogany skin and the strong, masculine features they'd both inherited from their father. A prominent tort attorney, Marcus had been enjoying the carefree lifestyle of a renowned ladies' man—until he went to Washington, D.C., four years ago and got tamed by Samara Layton.

As Marcus plucked Matt out of his brother's arm, Michael swung Malcolm over his head and onto his shoulders, making the boy squeal with delight. Marcus did the same with Matt, lest he feel cheated.

"Where's Samara?" Michael asked his brother as they started up the walk toward their father's house.

"Getting her hair done." Marcus smiled. "After a week of swimming and sweating out her hair at one theme park after another, she said she was in desperate need of a fresh relaxer. I told her to treat herself to a massage while she was at it, so we might not see her for a long time."

Michael gave his brother an amused sidelong glance. "What a kind, thoughtful husband you are."

Marcus shrugged. "What can I say? Nothing but the best for my queen."

If the comment had been made by anyone else, Michael might have rolled his eyes in laughing disbelief. But he knew better than anyone how much Marcus loved Samara. He worshipped the ground she walked on and would do anything for her. So when he called her his queen, Michael knew he was speaking from the heart.

"Grandpa!"

Sterling Wolf was waiting in the doorway, an excited grin wreathing his face at the sight of his sons and grandchildren. As they drew nearer, he snapped a picture with the expensive digital camera he'd received as a gift last month on Father's Day.

"Beautiful," he pronounced, beaming with pride as he tucked the camera into the front pocket of his polo shirt. "You boys look just like your father and uncle did at your age."

Michael and Marcus had barely set down the twins before they rushed into their grandfather's wide-open arms. Sterling hugged them tightly, bellowing with laughter as they began babbling about their adventures at Disney World.

"Whoa," Marcus called out, raising his voice to be heard above the cacophony. "Grandpa can't understand a word you boys are saying. One at a time."

"Aw, leave 'em alone," Sterling said good-naturedly. "This is music to my ears."

Michael and Marcus exchanged amused glances. "Do you ever remember him saying that when *we* were growing up?" Marcus asked.

Michael grinned. "Nope."

Pointedly ignoring them, Sterling whispered conspiratorially to his grandsons, "Ms. Frizell has a special treat waiting for you in the kitchen. Why don't you go see what it is?"

With eager squeals, the boys took off down the hall in a flash of matching blue T-shirts and white sneakers. Sterling smiled as he watched them go, the epitome of the proud, doting grandfather. He'd wept with joy the day the twins were born—the first time in years Michael had seen his tough, hard-nosed father reduced to tears.

Heaving a deep sigh of contentment, Sterling turned to Michael and Marcus. "It's good to have the Wolf pack together again," he declared, draping an arm around each son's shoulder as they started for the foyer. "Thanks for coming over and spending your Saturday with your old man."

"You don't have to thank us, Dad," Marcus said, taking the

words out of Michael's mouth. "You know you're the main reason Samara and I decided to move back to Atlanta. We wanted to be closer to you, and we didn't want to deprive the boys of growing up around their grandfather."

"I sure do appreciate that," Sterling conceded earnestly. "The day you called to tell me that good news made me as happy as the day I found out your brother had strong-armed the network executives into letting him tape his show here instead of New York."

Michael chuckled. "I didn't 'strong-arm' anyone."

"Actually, you did," Marcus countered wryly. "When it was time to renegotiate your contract after the first year, you gave the producers an ultimatum. Either they relocated your set to Atlanta, or you walked. But not only did you threaten to walk, you told them you'd approach Ted Turner with the idea of using your show to launch a rival food network based in Atlanta. With *Howlin' Good* being such a huge ratings hit, you knew how badly your producers wanted to keep you, so you played hardball." His tone was laced with admiration. "And here I thought *I* was the ruthless lawyer in the family."

Michael and Sterling laughed.

When they reached the kitchen, they found the twins perched on high-backed stools at the center island, munching happily on cupcakes decorated with miniature Mickey Mouse ears. Their hands and mouths were smeared with purple frosting, and when they looked up and flashed chocolaty grins, everyone dissolved into laughter.

After settling down the twins with an animated movie, Marcus joined his father and Michael on the veranda. Flopping into a chair at the wrought-iron table, Marcus reached for one of the glasses of iced tea that had been poured for him.

"Good stuff," he declared after taking a long, appreciative sip. He sighed. "Another thing I missed about home—sweet tea. They don't know the first thing about brewing good

Southern tea in Washington. One of these days I'll have to ask Ms. Frizell what her secret ingredient is."

Sterling grunted. "Good luck with that. I've already tried, and she won't give it up."

Michael chuckled. "She adds a little baking soda. It acts as a preservative to keep the tea from becoming cloudy and bitter."

Marcus shook his head at Sterling. "Shoulda known she'd tell *him*. The chefs always stick together."

"Of course." Michael grinned.

"So how's Lexi?" Sterling asked him. "Talk to her lately?"

"Doesn't he always?" Marcus interjected with a grin.

Michael frowned. "What's that supposed to mean?"

"I believe your brother's trying to imply that you and Lexi never go a day without talking to each other," Sterling explained.

"So? What's wrong with that? She's one of my closest friends."

"Right," Marcus said drily. "And it never occurred to you that she might want to be more than just a friend to you."

Michael rolled his eyes. "Of course it occurred to me. The first time we met was at a party where everyone we knew was paired off into couples." Inwardly he smiled at the memory of the sloppy, drunken kiss he and Lexi had shared, the sparks that failed to ignite between them. In the ensuing years, she'd become that female friend every guy should have—the one he went to for dating advice and to get a woman's perspective on the female psyche. In all the time they'd been friends, not once had Michael suspected that Lexi was secretly carrying a torch for him. He knew she wasn't.

Marcus seemed hell-bent on proving otherwise. "She's never liked any of your girlfriends—"

"Neither has Dad."

"—and she never misses an opportunity to tell you why she thinks someone is wrong for you."

"Again, neither does Dad. That's what people who care about you are supposed to do."

"All right," Marcus said, pinning his brother with a direct gaze. "Since you've got an answer for everything, here's something else for you to consider. Lexi's marriage only lasted two years. Why do you think that is?"

Michael met his gaze steadily. "Not everyone can be as lucky as you and Samara."

"Ain't that the truth," Sterling murmured.

Michael and Marcus fell silent, suddenly reminded of the way their parents' marriage had ended in bitter divorce after their mother was caught cheating on Sterling. Although Michael had made peace with her long ago, he'd never forgotten how her infidelity had torn their family apart. Seeing their father reduced to a shell of his former self had taken such an emotional toll on Michael and Marcus that they'd both vowed they would never get married or have children.

Marcus had had a change of heart.

Michael didn't think he ever would.

Leaning back in his chair, Marcus said quietly, "You're right, Mike. Samara's the best thing that ever happened to me, and not a day goes by that I don't count my blessings. I guess what I've been trying to get at is that it's not too late for you." He glanced at his father. "For either of you."

Sterling guffawed. "I'm too damn old to be bothered with all that."

"No, you're not," Marcus protested.

"Trust me, boy, I am. But your brother isn't." Sterling cut a sideways grin at Michael. "Back to what we were discussing before—"

Michael held up a hand. "There's nothing going on between me and Lexi. We're just friends, and that's all we're ever gonna be."

Seeing the look that passed between his father and Marcus, Michael felt a surge of irritation. Pushing back his chair, he stood and walked over to the railing that wrapped around the veranda.

New visitors to the house always gushed over the sprawling backyard, which boasted a gazebo, a guesthouse, a small pool and a series of garden beds that added vibrant splashes of color to the landscape. A surrounding canopy of trees kept out the scorching summer heat and gave the yard an air of seclusion. In a glowing feature article published several years ago, *Better Homes and Gardens* had described the yard as an "architectural paradise" and "a slice of heaven to rival Callaway Gardens"—lines that Sterling couldn't resist quoting to anyone who visited the house.

Not surprisingly, the backyard was the family's favorite gathering place, playing host to summer cookouts, pool parties, birthday parties, scavenger hunts for the twins and—most memorable of all—Marcus's wedding. Michael couldn't help smiling at a mental image of Samara, a vision in white wafting down a rose-strewn aisle in the picturesque garden. If the day hadn't been so profoundly special, Michael might have teased his brother about the tears that had streamed freely down his face as he'd gazed upon his bride. But the truth was that even Michael had gotten choked up during the ceremony. And in the deep, dark recesses of his heart, he'd wondered if he would ever get his own fairy-tale ending.

"So what's going on between you and that doctor you were arguing with the other day?" Sterling asked, breaking into Michael's thoughts.

Michael frowned. Just when he'd fooled himself into believing he could go an entire hour without thinking about Reese St. James.

He turned, arms folded across his chest as he glared balefully at his father. Undaunted, Sterling grinned like the proverbial cat that ate the canary.

"What doctor?" Marcus demanded, looking from one to the other. "What'd I miss?"

"Nothing," Michael grumbled.

"Plenty," Sterling said at the same time.

A slow, knowing grin crawled across Marcus's face. "I'll take your word for it, Dad. So what happened?"

"Well, on Wednesday I overheard an argument between—"

Michael snorted. "*Overheard?* Pops, you were eavesdropping."

Sterling looked disgruntled. "It ain't eavesdropping—"

"—if the conversation takes place under your roof," Michael and Marcus finished, then laughed. How many times had their father used that line to justify eavesdropping on their phone conversations when they were growing up? He'd given the same rationale for snooping through their belongings to make sure they weren't hiding any drugs, though he'd always assured them that someday they would thank him for his vigilance. The Wolf brothers were the only kids in the neighborhood who'd been subjected to random drug testing until they left home for college.

"As I was saying," Sterling continued pointedly, "I *overheard* an argument between Mike and a woman he'd met at the restaurant. Apparently he'd ticked her off pretty good by accusing her of impersonating a food critic."

"*What?*" Marcus's surprised gaze swung to his brother. "Why'd you do something like that?"

Biting back an impatient oath, Michael quickly and succinctly explained what had happened that Tuesday night, glossing over the kiss he and Reese had shared. When he'd finished his account, Marcus shook his head in amused disbelief.

"Is she unattractive?" he asked.

"Far from it," Michael grudgingly admitted.

"Then why would you even think she'd have to resort to a stunt like that?"

"Like I said," Michael ground out, "it was an honest mistake, one that could have happened to anyone. Anyway, it doesn't matter now. She got her revenge."

"How so?" Sterling and Marcus asked in unison.

Michael smiled grimly. "She's going to be my new apprentice."

His father and brother listened with rapt attention as he told them about the riveting audition performance that had made Reese a shoo-in to win the competition. By the time he'd finished describing her sassy comedic shtick, both men were laughing uproariously.

"Man, I wish I could've been there to see it," Marcus said.

"Me, too," Sterling agreed. "That young lady sounds like quite a pistol."

"Oh, she is," Michael muttered as a memory of glittering, defiant eyes flashed though his mind. And the mouth on her. He couldn't remember the last time he'd been both infuriated and aroused while sparring with a woman. "She's definitely going to be a handful."

Marcus gave him a knowing grin. "Think you're up for the challenge?"

"Of course," Michael said, thinking, *God help me if I'm wrong!*

Chapter 7

Reese drew a deep, fortifying breath, then raised her hand and pressed the doorbell. As she waited for a response, her heart hammered so hard she thought it might bulldoze its way right out of her chest. Not for the first time that morning, she questioned the sanity of what she was doing. She must be crazy for coming here like this, uninvited. Maybe she should just—

A scrape of movement inside the apartment forestalled any thoughts of escape.

Then suddenly the door opened.

Michael stood there in a sleeveless white T-shirt and dark pajama bottoms, his long feet bare. Dark stubble covered his jaw, and his eyes were heavy lidded and bleary. He squinted down at her for a long moment, then closed his eyes as if he expected her to be gone when he reopened them.

Which, of course, she wasn't.

"Good morning," she said cheerfully.

"What time is it?" His voice was a low, husky rasp that made her stomach clench.

"It's, um, nine o'clock," she answered sheepishly.

He cursed under his breath and closed his eyes again, this time looking as if he were trying to find his center of gravity. When he reached up and scrubbed his hands over his face, his thick, muscular biceps bunched and flexed with the movement.

Reese gulped. Hard.

After another interminable moment, those dark eyes slanted open and refocused on her face. He looked so big and menacing framed in the doorway that for a moment Reese felt like a hapless camper who'd wandered too far into the forest and awakened a bear from winter hibernation.

"What the hell," he growled, "are you doing here?"

Ungluing her tongue from the roof of her mouth, Reese thrust a covered cup at him. "I brought you coffee."

He stared at the cup in her hand, making no move to take it. "Coffee," he echoed flatly.

She nodded. "From a gourmet coffee shop near Layla's house. It's pretty good, though not as good as the coffee I make. Next time I'll bring you some of mine," she added, drawing his eyes from the cup to her face.

One heavy brow winged upward. "Next time?"

"Sure." She smiled bravely.

His gaze roamed over her, from head to toe and slowly back up again. After another moment, he reached out and accepted the proffered cup from her hand. As their fingers brushed, heat sizzled through her veins.

They stared at each other.

Unconsciously Reese licked her lips, and watched his hooded eyes follow the path of her tongue. "Aren't you going to invite me inside?" she asked, a touch breathless.

Michael hesitated, then staggered aside to open the door wider for her. As she stepped past him, her shoulder grazed the iron slabs of his chest. Her breasts tingled, and her pulse drummed erratically.

Ignoring her body's reaction to him—no easy feat—she advanced into the foyer and swept a look around. The stunning two-story penthouse featured Italian marble floors, elegant crown molding, ultramodern lighting and solid, contemporary furnishings done in masculine earth tones. Just off the main living area was a dramatic floating staircase that wound to an upper level. There were walls of nothing but windows that revealed spectacular views of Buckhead and, in the distance, downtown Atlanta.

The luxurious penthouse transcended the definition of a bachelor pad. It was a showplace—and immaculate to boot.

Reese whistled softly. "Wow. This is quite a crib you have."

Behind her, Michael grunted something unintelligible.

Smiling, she turned in time to catch him checking out her butt in the formfitting jeans she wore. The hungry gleam in his eyes sent another rush of tingling heat through her body.

Pretending not to notice what he'd been doing, she grinned playfully at him. "I thought you might live in one of those McMansions that Buckhead is famous for."

A shadow of a smile touched his lips, softening his features. "I don't need all that space. I spend more time at the restaurant and my father's house than here."

"Which would explain why the place is spotless. You're never home."

"Exactly." He raised the cup to his mouth and took a long sip. As he swallowed, his eyes closed in an expression of ecstasy that made her envy the coffee.

"Good?" There was a husky catch to her voice.

He nodded slowly. "Very."

She cleared her throat. "I didn't take you for one of those artsy-fartsy gourmet coffee lovers. So I just stuck with something basic. Something dark and strong."

"You done good," he drawled.

Reese warmed with pleasure, which made her feel like the world's biggest idiot. "I'm sorry. It didn't even occur to me that you might be at church this morning...or entertaining company."

His eyes glittered with amusement. "Are you asking me if I had a woman over last night?"

She shook her head quickly. "Of course not. That's none of my business." Yet she couldn't suppress a stab of jealousy at the thought of him spending a long, steamy night between the legs of some faceless female.

"You're right. It's none of your business." He shuffled past her, sipping his coffee. "But since you obviously want to know—"

"I don't—"

"—I was at the restaurant until six in the morning finalizing preparations for an event I'm catering next week. I was hoping to sleep in late," he added with a sardonic glance over his shoulder.

"Oh." Reese bit her bottom lip, feeling guilty. "Sorry."

After less than three hours of sleep, Michael should have looked like death warmed over. Instead his bed-rumpled appearance only added to his virile sexiness. And was there *anything* the man didn't look good wearing? As if his powerful biceps weren't mouthwatering enough in that sleeveless T-shirt, now she couldn't take her eyes off the way his pajama bottoms clung to his round, well-toned butt. She imagined digging her nails into those clenching and unclenching muscles, urging him deeper as he thrust into her. The image was so vivid, so explicitly carnal, that her loins throbbed in wanton response.

Mesmerized, she followed him into the enormous living room, more than a little disappointed when he sank down heavily on the sofa, cutting off her view of that amazing ass. Leaning his head back against the sofa, he regarded her tiredly for a moment, his lids at half mast. Like he was fighting to keep his eyes open.

Reese felt another pang of guilt. She, who'd never known the meaning of the word *impulsive* until she met this man, had chosen the worst possible day to act on a spontaneous urge.

"You never did answer my question," Michael murmured.

"Which one?" Reese asked, sitting on a chair upholstered in sumptuous brown leather.

"What, exactly, are you doing here?"

"I told you. I wanted to bring you coffee." She smiled whimsically. "I'm trying to get into my new role as your apprentice."

"Yeah?" He sounded amused. "You gonna pick up my dry-cleaning, too?"

"I wouldn't go *that* far."

His answering smile, the first real one he'd allowed since her arrival, made her heart lurch crazily. "Can't blame a guy for trying," he teased.

Her smile widened. "No, I guess not."

As he raised the cup to his mouth and drank more coffee, her gaze was drawn to his right forearm, which bore a distinct tattoo that identified him as an Omega Psi Phi fraternity member.

"How'd you find my address and get inside the building?"

Reese's eyes snapped back to his face, and she grinned. "Your address was on the contract I had to sign for the show. As for getting into the building, I flirted shamelessly with the doorman, made him think I was one of your newest playthings." She paused, arching a brow. "He must get that a lot. It was almost too easy."

Michael shook his head, mouth twitching. "I plead the Fifth."

Reese laughed. "I bet you do, Que-Dog."

He glanced down at his tattooed arm, then laughed.

Moments later, when they were still smiling companionably at each other, she murmured, "See, it's working already."

"What is?"

"My plan." At his wary look, she elaborated, "I came over here this morning hoping we could reach a truce."

"A truce," Michael repeated slowly.

She nodded. "I thought it might be good for us to spend some time getting to know each other better, so we won't be at each other's throats when taping begins next week. I know how important it is for us to have chemistry."

He looked amused. "I think we've already established that we have chemistry. If we had any more, we'd both have to be hosed down."

Reese blushed, her belly quivering at his words. "I'm not talking about *that* kind of chemistry."

"Why not? It's the only kind of chemistry worth talking about. If you don't believe me, I'd be more than happy to remind you." He wiggled his brows suggestively.

Reese laughed, even as she felt a responsive twitch between her thighs. "That won't be necessary. Besides, just a minute ago you were swaying on your feet and could barely keep your eyes open!"

A slow, wolfish grin curved his mouth. "I'm wide awake now. Just say the word, sweetheart, and I'm all yours."

Oh God. Reese nearly vaulted out of the chair and into his lap. She wanted him, wanted him with every cell in her body, every fiber of her being. It took a monumental act of willpower for her to remain seated, to resist the wicked gleam in his eyes that was pure temptation.

Sitting back and crossing her legs—to stop the vibrations in her clitoris and to appear composed—she tsk-tsked and wagged her finger at him. "Now, Mr. Wolf, is that any way to talk to your new apprentice?"

"Depends on what kind of apprentice you wanna be," he drawled lazily. "Instruction doesn't have to be limited to the kitchen."

Her insides clenched at the unmistakable implication. Smiling coquettishly, she purred, "Who says I need instruction—in *or* out of the kitchen?"

Michael stared at her for an arrested moment, his grin faltering. When she batted her eyelashes at him, he let out a low, rough chuckle and shook his head, looking slightly dazed. "You're gonna be the death of me, woman."

Swallowing a grin, Reese deadpanned, "I hope not. I was just starting to like you again."

He threw back his head and laughed, the sound so warm and infectious she couldn't help joining in.

When their mirth had subsided, Michael set his coffee cup on a side table and rose from the sofa, no longer unsteady on his feet.

"Where are you going?" Reese asked him.

"To take a shower—a very cold one. And then I'm gonna get dressed and show you around my beautiful city."

Her eyes widened as a wave of astonished pleasure swept through her. "Really? You'd give up your Sunday to take me sightseeing?"

"Sure, why not? You brought me coffee."

"I can make you breakfast, too," Reese called after him as he started from the room.

He paused, glancing over his shoulder at her. He looked so surprised and touched by the offer that Reese wondered whether he'd gotten so used to cooking for others that no one ever bothered to cook for him.

"You know what?" he said softly. "I'm definitely gonna take you up on that. But can I get a rain check?"

"Of course." She smiled shyly. "Do you want to just stop somewhere on the way out?"

"Yeah. And I know just the place."

The Sunday jazz brunch at Wolf's Soul was the place to be.

Locals and tourists alike flocked to the restaurant every weekend for an award-winning buffet that included everything from eggs Benedict to crawfish étouffée, along with a toe-tapping dose of live jazz music served up by the *Howlin' Good* band. Kids ate free, while college students and senior citizens enjoyed half-price discounts.

All proceeds from the brunch helped to fund nonprofit organizations that benefited Atlanta's inner-city youth, who were near and dear to Michael's heart. He mentored at-risk teens, gave them jobs at his restaurant and regularly had them in his studio audience. Two years ago his alma nater, Morehouse College, had established the Michael Wolf scholarship for economically disadvantaged students. Given Michael's commitment to his community, it was no wonder Atlantans had proudly embraced him as their native son.

An hour after arriving at Wolf's Soul with Michael, Reese pushed away her empty plate and sighed deeply. "That was absolutely wonderful."

"I'm glad you enjoyed it," Michael said, lounging across from her at a small table located on a second-story balcony that overlooked Peachtree Street. Music from inside the restaurant drifted through the double French doors, a lazy blues instrumental. The morning sun hadn't cranked up the temperature yet, so sitting outdoors was tolerable, even pleasant.

Reese sighed again. Filled with good food and nursing her second mimosa, she felt relaxed and deliciously content. She could have stayed there, with Michael, for the rest of the day.

He smiled, watching her with a look of quiet satisfaction, as he'd done throughout their meal. "Can I get you anything else?"

Reese laughed. "Are you kidding? I couldn't eat another bite."

His dark eyes glinted at her. "Are you sure? Our chocolate fountain is *very* popular."

She groaned, rubbing her full stomach. "I'm sure it is. But if I go anywhere near it, I'm going to explode. God knows I've already eaten way more than I should have." She shot him an accusing look. "I blame you."

His expression was one of exaggerated innocence. "Me?"

"Yes, *you.* You're the one who kept urging me to try this, and try that. And everything sounded so good I just couldn't resist. Like that brioche French toast, and the crab cake Benedict. And that sweet potato hash. Mmm, positively divine. Anyway," she said pointedly, before she got off track, "after all that food we just ate, you have no business even *mentioning* that chocolate fountain to me. What are you—a sadist?"

Michael laughed, lazily running his finger around the rim of his champagne glass. "I like watching you eat. You take pleasure in food in a way that any chef would appreciate. There's nothing worse than pouring your heart and soul into a meal, only to watch someone pick over it because they're on a diet, or they don't wanna mess up their lipstick, or they're afraid to look greedy if they clean their plate and ask for seconds." His eyes twinkled with humor. "You know how you women do."

Reese grinned. "I would say you need to stop cooking for such ungrateful wenches, but I seriously doubt you've ever had to worry about anyone picking over food *you've* made."

"You'd be surprised."

"Well, if *I'm* ever privileged enough to have you cook for me, I promise to bring a big appetite."

Michael smiled. "And I promise to leave you satisfied."

Reese's mouth went dry. For a moment she just stared at him, wondering if they were talking about food or lovemaking. Either way, there was no doubt in her mind that Michael knew his way around a woman's body the way he did a gourmet kitchen.

Holding his gaze, she reached for her glass and held it up. "A toast," she said. "To good food."

"And endless possibilities," Michael added silkily, quickening her heart rate.

They clinked glasses and sipped their drinks, staring at each other like they were the only two people in the world. They might as well have been.

Though the restaurant was filled to capacity, they were the only occupants of the small balcony. Reese didn't know whether this was by accident or design. She didn't care. She liked having Michael to herself, though she'd certainly enjoyed watching his interactions with customers when they'd first arrived. He'd gone out of his way to greet as many people as he could, shaking hands, answering questions, hugging elderly grandmothers and coaxing smiles out of babies. Watching him in action, Reese realized that money and fame had not changed him. He'd never forgotten where he came from, and his customers loved him for it.

"Coming here for breakfast was a brilliant idea," Reese murmured.

"I'm glad you feel that way." Michael smiled ruefully. "After the way I behaved the other night, I was afraid you'd never want to come near this place again."

"I wasn't planning to, believe me." She chuckled. "I was so mad at you, I even thought about burning your cookbook."

He shouted with laughter. "Damn, baby, that's cold!"

Reese grinned wickedly. "Hot, you mean. As in, torched to ashes."

Michael shook his head at her, his eyes glimmering with amusement and respect. "You are one formidable woman, Reese St. James. Remind me never to cross you again."

She laughed, sipping her mimosa. As she crossed her legs under the table, Michael shifted at the same time. Without warning her foot collided with his firm, muscled calf, sending jolts of sensation shooting up her leg to her loins.

Their gazes locked, a current of pure sexual awareness passing between them.

"So *this* is where you're hiding!" boomed a deep male voice threaded with laughter.

Michael swore under his breath, staring past Reese with an expression of annoyance mingled with dread.

Curious, she glanced around and saw a man coming toward them with a cocky swagger that could only be rivaled by Michael's. The stranger was dressed in a well-tailored charcoal suit, his debonair appearance offset by the toothpick dangling insolently from a corner of his mouth.

As he reached their table, his speculative gaze took inventory of Reese's flushed cheeks and Michael's scowl before a knowing grin spread across his face.

"What's up, Wolfman?" he greeted Michael, clapping him on the back. "No wonder your waiters were being so tight-lipped about where you were. You're up here having a hot date. And speaking of hot…" He eyed Reese with frank male interest, his full lips curving in a smile that had undoubtedly seduced more than a few women into parting with their panties. "Hello, beautiful."

Reese couldn't help smiling back. "Hello."

Grudgingly Michael performed the introductions. "Reese, I'd like you to meet Quentin Reddick. Q, this is Reese St. James."

"It's a real pleasure to meet you, Reese." Quentin held her hand a little longer than was necessary, earning a scowl from Michael.

While both men were tall, wide-shouldered and incredibly good-looking, the similarities ended there. Where Michael was dark and smoldering, Quentin had a golden complexion and bright hazel eyes that sparkled with irrepressible mischief.

"So tell me something, Reese," he drawled. "Where's Mike been hiding you?"

She grinned. "Actually, he hasn't. I'm visiting from Houston."

"Visiting Mike?"

"Not exactly." She paused. "I'm going to be his new apprentice on *Howlin' Good*."

"Is that right?" Quentin slanted a knowing grin at Michael. "You sly, sly dog."

Michael glared at him. "Don't you have someplace else to be?"

His grin widened. "Not at the moment. I just came from church and decided to swing by my favorite restaurant to get my eat on." He winked at Reese. "Best places to meet beautiful single women—the Lord's house and Wolf's Soul."

Reese chuckled. "Good to know you've got your priorities straight."

"Always." His gaze roamed across her face. "So, what do you do down there in Houston?"

Michael rolled his eyes in exasperation. "What's up with the interrogation, Q?"

"It's all right." Reese smiled at Quentin. "I'm a doctor."

"A doctor, huh?" His expression turned downright roguish. "Maybe you can help me out with this little problem I've been having. See, I—"

"She's an ob-gyn," Michael told him smugly.

"*She is?*" Quentin had the decency to look embarrassed. "Damn. Never mind."

Michael and Reese laughed.

Deciding to turn the tables on Quentin, Reese asked, "So what do *you* do for a living?"

"Nothing as noble as what you do," he answered, lazily dipping his hands into his pockets. "I'm just a lawyer."

"Q is a managing partner at my brother's law firm," Michael elaborated.

Quentin winked at Reese. "Marcus was the only one in this town crazy enough to hire me."

Michael chuckled drily, shaking his head at Reese. "As much as I'd like to agree with him, he's being modest—which is rare. The truth is, he was working at one of the biggest law firms in the country when my brother lured him away. Marcus considers Quentin a real asset to his company."

"I'm impressed." Reese smiled at Quentin. "Would you like to sit down?"

"No," Michael said flatly.

"Sure," Quentin replied at the same time.

They stared each other down. Or rather, Michael glowered while Quentin looked unabashedly amused.

Biting the inside of her cheek to keep from laughing at their standoff, Reese said, "Don't mind him, Quentin. Please pull up a chair and join us."

He did, flashing a triumphant grin at Michael as he sat right next to Reese. She decided not to read too much into Michael's narrowed eyes and clenched jaw.

"How long have you guys known each other?" she asked, dividing a curious glance between both men.

"Mike and I go way back," Quentin drawled, stretching out his long legs as he settled more comfortably into the chair.

"We grew up in the same neighborhood, went to Morehouse together. Pledged the same fraternity."

"Another Omega man, huh?" Reese gave him a whimsical smile. "So you're Q the Que."

He grinned. "Yep, that's what they called me." A wicked gleam lit his eyes. "We called Mike the Wolfman, and not just because of his last name, either. You know that howl he does on his TV show, the famous howl that his fans go crazy over? Well, he's been doing that for over twenty years. Wanna know how it got started?"

"She doesn't need to know that," Michael cut in brusquely.

"Oh, but I *want* to," Reese countered. "I happen to really enjoy that howl, and if there's an interesting story behind it, I'd like to hear it."

Michael didn't blink. "No."

Quentin winked conspiratorially at Reese. "I'll tell you later."

"Like hell you will," Michael growled, leveling a glare at his friend that promised violent retribution if Quentin defied him.

"On second thought, baby girl, it's probably better that you *don't* know." Quentin's grave tone was belied by the mischief twinkling in his hazel eyes. "I wouldn't want to offend your feminine sensibilities."

Reese laughed. "That bad, huh?"

"That *good,* you mean." Quentin sighed nostalgically, drawing a dirty look from Michael.

Reese grinned. She could easily envision the two friends ruling campus parties, along with a pack of rowdy, high-stepping fraternity brothers who rushed the dance floor every time "Atomic Dog" blared over the speakers. With their good looks and killer smiles, Michael and Quentin must have had their way with the ladies. No doubt they still did.

Michael looked relieved when one of his busboys appeared to clear their table and to tell him that his sous chef wanted his advice on wine pairings for tonight's house specialty.

"Go on and handle your business," Quentin urged, waving Michael off. "I'll keep Reese company while you're gone."

"Hell, no," Michael growled, rounding the table.

Before Reese could react, he grabbed her hand, tugged her out of the chair and dragged her downstairs with him.

They spent the rest of the day sightseeing around Atlanta.

Their first stop was the Martin Luther King, Jr. National Historic Site, where they toured the civil rights leader's birth home, former church and neighborhood. As they strolled the beautifully landscaped grounds of Peace Plaza and walked around the King Center, people recognized Michael and pointed him out excitedly to their companions. But for the most part they kept a respectful distance, perhaps in deference to the solemn locale.

Later, as Reese and Michael stood beside the clear reflecting pool that surrounded Dr. King's marble tomb, she was so moved that tears welled in her eyes and ran down her cheeks.

Wordlessly Michael pulled a handkerchief from his pocket and passed it to her.

She let out a teary laugh as she dabbed at her eyes. "Only a true Southern gentleman would carry around a hankie in his jeans."

Michael smiled softly. "I came prepared."

She sniffed. "So you knew I'd be reduced to a blubbering idiot if we came here?"

"You wouldn't be the first. As many times as I've been here, I'm always moved by the experience. Believe me, you have nothing to be embarrassed about."

His gentle words earned him a grateful, albeit wobbly smile. Reese held up the damp wad of handkerchief. "I'm gonna hang on to this—just in case."

Michael chuckled softly. "It's yours." He reached out, his

knuckle gently skimming her cheek as he tucked an errant strand of hair behind her ear.

Reese stared up at him, arrested by the tender expression on his face. When their eyes caught and held, her heart thundered.

After a prolonged moment Michael stepped back, clearing his throat and glancing around at everything but her. "Ready to go?"

She let out a shaky breath, then nodded.

They left the historic black neighborhood and returned to Midtown to visit the High Museum of Art. The popular museum was housed in a striking contemporary building that featured four floors of European and American paintings, decorative artifacts, photography, graphics and an impressive collection of African art. Unlike Victor, Michael didn't sigh impatiently or complain as Reese wandered from one exhibit to another, sometimes lingering for long stretches of time. He seemed to take quiet pleasure in her spirited enjoyment of the museum. When they stopped for an early dinner in the piazza, he gave her his undivided attention as she enthused about her favorite artists and explained how a college professor had turned her on to the Renaissance period.

"That's another reason I'm dying to visit Italy," she told Michael. "To see the works of Michelangelo and da Vinci, to visit Florence Cathedral and St. Peter's Basilica." She sighed wistfully. "One of these days."

"What's stopping you?" Michael asked curiously. "You're a doctor, so it can't be the money."

"No, it's not that." She bit her lip, remembering with renewed irritation that were it not for Victor, she could be in Venice right now.

"So what is it?" Michael probed, watching her with a quiet, focused intensity that made her wonder if he'd somehow discerned her thoughts.

She heaved another sigh. "I don't know. Growing up, I'd always intended to travel a lot, see the world. But after college there was med school, then my residency. Once I started working at the hospital, time just got away from me." She shrugged. "I guess we all have to make sacrifices to achieve our goals."

"That's true," Michael murmured, and she wondered about the personal sacrifices he must have made along the way to becoming an international celebrity.

Before she could ask, he said suddenly, "Why are you on sabbatical?"

Reese tensed. "What do you mean?"

"You're only thirty-four. So I'm guessing you haven't been practicing medicine long enough to be burned out. So what would make you take a two-month hiatus from a job you obviously love?"

Reese stared into his keen dark eyes, dismayed by his perceptiveness. She thought of not answering him, but somehow she knew he wouldn't let her get away with that.

"I lost one of my patients in childbirth," she said dully.

His expression softened. "I'm sorry to hear that. When did it happen?"

"Two months ago."

He nodded slowly. "You blame yourself." At her surprised look, he gently explained, "You didn't say one of your patients had died in childbirth. You said you lost a patient, as if it were your fault."

Reese swallowed hard, wanting to close her eyes against his intense scrutiny. "I did everything I could to save her."

"Of course." He wasn't patronizing her. He'd spoken with absolute certainty, as though there was no room for doubt regarding her innocence. "So what happened?"

It was the tender concern in his voice that broke her. The raw emotions she'd been holding in check welled up inside her and spilled out: the grief, the guilt, the frustration over her inability to convince Deidra Thomas that she had too many risk factors to have another baby. By the time Reese finished blurting out everything, Michael had brought his chair around to hers and pulled her into his arms. As she quietly sobbed into his chest, he stroked her back and murmured soothingly to her.

It didn't matter to Reese that they were in public. His arms were strong, his voice was understanding and she'd needed a good shoulder to cry on for far too long.

Still, she felt a little embarrassed when she finally pulled away and met the sympathetic stares of several other diners, many of whom had asked for Michael's autograph when he and Reese first arrived. What must those people be thinking now?

Reese fumbled out the handkerchief Michael had given her earlier and mopped at her streaming eyes. "I knew this would come in handy again," she joked with a whispery laugh.

Michael smiled, kissing the top of her head.

"God, I didn't mean to cause a scene." She blew her nose, glancing around furtively. "I hope there aren't any paparazzi around. They'll run an exposé about a woman reduced to hysterical tears after you broke up with her."

Michael chuckled. "I never do breakups over a meal. It's sacrilegious." He ran a thumb under her eye, wiping at the moisture she'd missed.

She gave him a rueful smile. "I assure you that I'm not always this weepy."

"There's nothing wrong with having a good cry. And you definitely needed one." He put a finger under her chin and lifted it. His gentle eyes searched hers. "Feel any better?"

"I do," Reese admitted, surprised. "That was very… cathartic."

In a moment of clarity, she'd decided to donate her grand prize money to Deidra Thomas's family. It wouldn't bring back Deidra, but the hundred thousand dollars would help cover the family's medical expenses and would enable Ian Thomas to start a college fund for little Faith.

Reese touched Michael on the shoulder. "Thank you for loaning this to me."

He smiled into her eyes. "Anytime."

Seeking to lighten the mood, she picked up her wineglass and smiled at him. "So getting back to our original conversation. How many times have *you* been to Italy?"

He chuckled, not leaving her side. "How do you know I have?"

She gave him a look. "Any chef worth his knives has been there. So come on, Michael. Tell me all about it. Let me live vicariously through you."

He smiled again, and she listened with rapt absorption as he told her about his forays to Italy over the years. When he casually mentioned owning a small cottage in Tuscany, Reese groaned with envy and jokingly lobbied to have the apprentice episodes shot from that location—which Michael didn't think was such a bad idea.

When they left the museum, he surprised her by asking, "Have you ever played paintball?"

She laughed. "Not since childhood."

He flashed a wicked grin. "Then you're long overdue."

Reese snorted. "You're kidding, right?"

"Nope. And I know just the place. It's usually closed to the public on Sundays, but they're running a summer special."

"Great," Reese said weakly.

He winked at her. "It'll be fun."

He took her to a place called Paintball Atlanta. In exchange for two tickets to a live taping of *Howlin' Good,* the manager gave Michael and Reese their own private field, and they spent the next two hours chasing each other around with loaded paintball guns. Michael was fast, hunting Reese down with a stealth that any Navy SEAL would admire. She found herself alternately squealing with laughter and howling with frustration every time she got hit—which was often. Whenever she *did* manage to pick him off, she was so ecstatic that she didn't even care that he'd probably let his guard down just to level the playing field.

It was the most fun she'd had in years. Afternoon stretched into night, and all too soon Michael was driving her home and walking her to the front door.

"I had a wonderful time," Reese said warmly, her sandals dangling from her fingertips. On the way to the paintball complex, they'd stopped at an outlet mall so she could get more appropriate footwear. Before she could even *think* about pulling out her credit card, Michael had paid for the new sneakers and strolled out the door, whistling cheerfully to drown out her protests.

He'd paid for everything, making their day together feel almost like a…date.

By far the best date she'd ever had in her life.

She blushed at the thought. "Thank you for giving up your entire Sunday to take me sightseeing. I know you probably would've preferred to stay home and catch up on sleep," she added ruefully.

Michael smiled down at her. "Sleep is overrated."

Ignoring the way her heart fluttered, she gave him a teasing grin. "You probably won't think so tonight when you're knocked out cold and drooling into your pillow."

He chuckled softly. "I don't drool."

Speak for yourself, Reese mused, staring at his full, sensual lips and remembering how incredible they'd felt against her own. The memory of that searing, soul-shattering kiss they'd shared would haunt her long after she'd returned to Texas.

Inexplicably, the thought of going home made her throat tighten.

"So," Michael drawled, "what're you doing tomorrow?"

"Sleeping."

They both laughed quietly, calmly, never taking their eyes off each other.

A sultry breeze kicked up, caressing Reese's skin. She wished it were Michael's hands, his mouth. She wanted nothing more than to invite him inside, to spend the night making love to him. But she knew she couldn't. Not until she'd decided what to do about Victor.

"When you're done sleeping tomorrow," Michael said, smiling, "maybe I could pick you up and take you to the studio. You know, to give you a tour and introduce you to the crew before we start taping next week."

Reese nodded quickly, so excited at the prospect of spending more time with him that she would have agreed to accompany him *anywhere*. "I'd like that very much."

"Good." He hesitated, then reached out and brushed his thumb across the pulse beating at the base of her neck.

Reese shivered. Everything inside her went hot and sensitive.

His eyes met hers. "Paint," he explained.

She nodded. She had to fight the intense urge to capture his hand and draw his thumb slowly into her mouth. And she didn't want to stop at his thumb.

"Good night, Reese," he said huskily.

She swallowed hard. "Good night, Michael."

With one last lingering look at her, he turned and sauntered to his car, which he'd parked beside hers in the driveway. She stood watching as he climbed inside the low-slung Maybach and closed the door. The engine purred to life.

He met her gaze through the windshield. *Go inside*, he mouthed.

Reese obeyed without hesitation. After closing and locking the front door, she sagged against it and lifted a trembling hand to her throat, where her skin still burned from Michael's whisper-soft touch.

When she closed her eyes, she swore she heard her relationship with Victor flatlining.

Chapter 8

The next morning, Michael was awakened by his ringing cell phone. He grabbed it off the nightstand and checked caller ID. When he saw Reese's number, his heart gave an involuntary bump.

He pressed the talk button more eagerly than he'd have preferred. "Hey, you."

"Good morning." That soft, smoky voice spilled into his ear like sun-warmed honey. "I know it's only seven-thirty. Did I wake you?"

He smiled. "For the second day in a row, sunshine."

"Uh-oh." She sounded amused. "Has anyone ever told you that you're positively terrifying first thing in the morning?"

He chuckled softly. "I'm not a morning person. Especially if I'm operating on less than three hours of sleep," he added pointedly.

She laughed. "Touché."

His smile widened. He was enjoying this too damn much. "Actually, Reese, I was going to call you as soon as I woke up."

"You were?"

"Yeah. I wanted to see what— *Hello?*"

The line had gone dead.

Michael held the phone away from his ear and stared at it in bewildered disbelief. Had she just *hung up* on him? Or had they gotten disconnected?

Frowning, he quickly dialed her number.

When she answered the phone laughing, he had his answer.

"Sorry," she said, sounding anything but apologetic. "I just couldn't resist."

"Of course you couldn't," Michael murmured, humor tugging at the corners of his lips. "I said I was going to call you, so you figured you'd let me do it. Clever."

"*I* thought so." She sighed contentedly.

He grinned wryly. "I see that *you're* a morning person."

She chuckled. "I'm a doctor. I'm used to getting calls at all hours of the night. Babies who decide to be born at 2:00 a.m. don't care whether or not I'm a morning person. So I've learned to adapt my moods. Any who," she continued cheerfully, "the reason I was calling was to find out what time you wanted to go to the studio. I have to run a few errands."

Run them tomorrow, Michael thought. *I've been dreaming about you all night and I can't wait to see you again. The sooner, the better.*

Aloud he said smoothly, "Take your time. We can go around eleven."

"Are you sure? I don't want to mess up your schedule."

"Nah, it's all good. I need to hit the gym for a couple hours, anyway."

She groaned. "That's what *I* should be doing. I need to burn off all that food you let me gorge on yesterday."

Michael grinned. He could think of at least one way he'd like to help her burn off calories—and it had nothing to do with the use of Nautilus equipment.

"You must spend a lot of time in the gym," she said appreciatively. "You're very…in shape."

He chuckled at the subtle compliment. "I played basketball

in high school and college. So, yeah, keeping fit is important to me. Especially since I'm surrounded by food all the time."

"Good point. Where do you work out?" she asked. "I might as well find a gym while I'm in town."

"There's a fitness center in my building. You're more than welcome to join me anytime."

"You're allowed guests?"

"Sure." At the thought of seeing her voluptuous body glistening with sweat after a good workout, his mouth watered and blood rushed straight to his groin. "You wanna come today?"

"Well…" she hedged.

He held his breath.

"No, that's okay. I'd better go ahead and take care of my errands. Besides," she added as an afterthought, "between sightseeing and playing paintball yesterday, we did a lot of walking and running. So that should tide me over for another day or two."

"Excuses, excuses," Michael teased.

She laughed. "I know, I know. But I'll be there with you in spirit."

She'd been "there" with him for the past six days. He couldn't get her out of his mind.

"I'll call you when I'm on my way," he told her.

"Sounds good. See you soon."

Not soon enough, Michael thought as he hung up the phone and set it on the nightstand.

Smiling, he clasped his hands behind his head and gazed up at the ceiling as images from yesterday tumbled through his mind. He remembered their incredibly romantic breakfast on the balcony at his restaurant. When he had introduced her to his staff afterward, he'd been fascinated by the way she'd laughed and chatted easily with everyone, charming the apron off his temperamental pastry chef and graciously accepting Griffin's profuse apologies for the mix-up with the food critic.

Reese had a way about her, an infectious warmth coupled

with an earthy sensuality that was utterly bewitching. As the day progressed, Michael had found himself falling deeper under her spell. By the time they'd finished shooting up each other with paintball guns—the most fun he'd ever had with a woman, bar none—he knew he was in trouble.

In the span of one day he'd gone from wishing he'd never laid eyes on her, to lamenting any time spent apart from her.

"Whoa," Michael whispered, shaken by the turn of his thoughts. He couldn't believe what was happening. Here it was barely eight o'clock in the morning, and he was lying in bed with a goofy smile on his face, obsessing over some woman he hardly even knew.

What the hell?

It was crazy. Totally out of character for him. He'd lost his damn mind.

Yet as he untangled himself from the covers and swung out of bed, he knew the extra spring in his step had everything to do with the fact that he'd be seeing Reese again soon.

And the sooner, the better.

But three and a half hours later when he pulled up to the now-familiar bungalow and saw a florist's delivery truck parked at the curb, he got a sinking feeling in his gut. And that was before he saw Reese standing in the doorway, her cell phone cradled between her ear and shoulder as she signed for the delivery. When the driver handed her a long white box tied with a red satin bow, she beamed with pleasure.

It was like a blow to Michael's chest.

He waited until the delivery truck had rumbled off before he climbed out of the car and slowly started up the walk. By the time he reached the front door, his good mood had completely disintegrated, replaced by a dark, seething emotion he didn't want to identify.

"Michael." Reese looked surprised to see him. Or maybe

guilty was a better word. "I thought you were going to call when you were on your way."

He'd been so eager to get there that he'd forgotten. Not that he was about to tell *her* that. "Since I said we could go around eleven," he said mildly, "I figured you'd be ready."

"I am. I just… Never mind." She opened the door wider and nervously gestured him inside.

As he stepped into the foyer, his gaze went immediately to a box of two dozen long-stemmed red roses that lay open on the table.

"Nice," Michael murmured, slowly removing his sunglasses. Roses were the kind of gift a guy sent to get himself out of the doghouse—or into a woman's bed. Unoriginal, but highly effective.

Reese wouldn't meet his gaze. "Yes, they are nice."

"For you?" *Please say no. Please say they came for your friend Layla.*

Reese hesitated, then reluctantly nodded. "Yes. They're mine."

His heart sank, though he should have known better than to get his hopes up. "So my hunch was right about you," he said, his voice pitched low.

Her hand fluttered to her throat. "What hunch?"

"I suspected that you might have a boyfriend. And you do."

She met his gaze then, but only for a moment before her eyes slid guiltily away. *Coward,* he silently mocked her.

Instead of answering him, she walked quickly to the table, saying, "I'm, uh, going to put these in water, then we can go."

As she scooped up the box of roses, a small white card floated to the floor. She didn't see it, so intent was she on beating a hasty retreat. As she continued to the kitchen, Michael bent down and picked up the card. Unable to resist, he read the typed message.

You didn't say I couldn't send roses. I miss you. Come back to me. Love, Victor.

Michael clenched his jaw as some strange new emotion washed over him—raw, fierce, primitive. Entirely foreign, entirely unwelcome.

He got slowly to his feet as Reese returned to the foyer, sucking her thumb where she'd presumably been pricked with a thorn. "Okay," she said briskly, "I'm ready to go."

Michael held up the card, and watched as a deep, embarrassed flush swept across her face. "It fell out of the box," he told her.

"Oh. Thanks," she muttered, practically snatching it out of his hand. She tapped it against her open palm for a moment, then looked up at him with an unspoken question in her eyes. Michael didn't have to guess what she was asking. She wanted to know whether he'd read the card.

He just looked at her, letting the tense silence hang between them.

Not surprisingly, she was the first to glance away. "We should probably go," she mumbled.

"You didn't answer my question," Michael said flatly.

She started away from him. "I left my handbag in the—"

"Did your boyfriend send the roses?"

"I don't—"

"Did he?" Michael demanded.

"Yes!" She rounded on him, those dark eyes flashing with fiery defiance. "Yes, the roses are from my boyfriend! His name is Victor. We've been together for over a year. We work at the same hospital. He loves my cooking. Anything else you want to know?"

"Yeah." Michael smirked, surprised by the strength of the jealousy he felt. "How does your *boyfriend* feel about you kissing other men?"

It was a low blow, and he knew it.

Reese flinched, hurt and anger flaring in her eyes. She took a step backward, glaring at him. "Maybe you should just leave," she said coldly.

"No," Michael snarled, his heart beating so savagely he

thought he might go into cardiac arrest at any moment. "I came to take you to the studio, and that's what I'm doing."

"Fine," she snapped. "Then I'm getting my damn purse."

"Fine. I'll wait in the damn car." He turned and stalked out of the house.

Reese joined him in the Maybach a few minutes later, slamming the door hard enough to make his teeth snap together. Without sparing her a glance he turned the ignition and gunned the accelerator, pinning her against the seat with a tight-knuckled grip on the door handle that gave him a perverse twinge of satisfaction.

He knew he was being irrational, that he had no right to feel so possessive over her. Yet he couldn't help himself. He wanted her, damn it. Wanted her like no other woman he'd ever wanted before. But as long as she had a boyfriend, she was completely off-limits to him. Because as much as Michael enjoyed playing the field, he'd always drawn the line at sleeping with women who were already taken. There were too many other fish in the sea for him to poach on another man's territory.

For years he'd despised Grant Rutherford for luring his mother away from Sterling. Grant hadn't respected Celeste's marriage or her responsibility to her family. He'd seen something he wanted and had gone after it, consequences be damned. As far as Michael was concerned, real men didn't go around stealing other people's wives. They found their own.

Given his personal convictions, it would be hypocritical of him to pursue Reese when he knew she was in a relationship. And if she cheated on her boyfriend, how could Michael ever trust her to be faithful to *him?*

Halfway to the downtown television studio, a burst of song from his cell phone cut through the frigid silence in the car. Out of the corner of his eye, Michael saw Reese raise a brow at the ring tone—"Fight the Power" by Public Enemy. It was his personal theme song for his brother, Marcus, the crusading lawyer.

In no mood for small talk, Michael snatched up the phone and growled, "Let me call you back later."

"Whoa." Marcus was taken aback. "Damn, what's wrong with *you?*"

Michael impatiently switched lanes. "This isn't a good time, little man."

"I'm sorry to hear that, because I need a favor."

"What?"

"Can you pick up Mom and Grant from the airport?"

"Tonight?"

"No." Marcus sounded puzzled. "What're you talking about? They're not arriving tonight."

Michael frowned. "When does their flight get in?"

"In an hour."

"*What?* Since when?"

"They changed their flight a couple weeks ago. Oh, yeah, that's right—you were on your book tour. I thought Dad told you."

"He must have forgot. Anyway, I'm on my way to the studio. Why can't you pick them up from the airport?"

"I had planned to," Marcus said grimly, "but I'm still at the office."

"Why? I thought you and Samara took another week off from work to spend time with the family."

"We did. But I had to come in to help put out a fire involving one of our big clients."

"What about Samara?" Samara Wolf was a public relations consultant, so her schedule was more flexible.

"She's out running around with her mother, finalizing preparations for the reception next Monday."

"Asha's already in town?" Michael asked in surprise. Her grand opening wasn't for another week.

"Yeah. She flew in yesterday afternoon. She was hoping to meet with you to discuss the reception menu, but you never answered your cell phone."

"I was out," Michael muttered with a sideways glance at Reese. She sat ramrod straight, her hands clasped tightly in her lap as she stared through the windshield, simmering with hostility.

"You turned off your phone yesterday?" Marcus asked.

Michael grunted an affirmative. He hadn't wanted the outside world to intrude on his time with Reese. *What a joke.*

"That must have been one helluva date," Marcus said slyly.

Michael scowled. "It wasn't a date." He felt rather than saw Reese stiffen even more in her seat.

"Whatever you say, bro." Marcus chuckled. "So can you swing by the airport, then drop Mom and Grant off at Dad's house?"

Yet another surprise. "Why aren't they staying with you and Samara like they always do?"

Marcus heaved a sigh. "You know Mom and Asha don't get along. It's like they're in competition with each other to see who can be the best grandmother. They're always one-upping each other with gifts for the twins, and Mom thinks Asha purposely scheduled the grand opening of her boutique to coincide with Mom's summer visit so *she* could steal the spotlight."

Michael rolled his eyes in exasperation. "Women and their drama."

"Tell me about it," Marcus agreed with a wry chuckle. "Needless to say, Samara and I didn't think having them under the same roof was such a good idea. So since Asha arrived first, she got dibs on accommodations."

Michael grinned. "Given the way she and Dad are always at each other's throats, staying with him was out of the question."

Marcus laughed. "You got that right. They'd probably kill each other before the week was over." A low murmur of voices could be heard in the background. "Listen, Mike, I gotta run. My client just arrived. Thanks for picking up Mom and Grant for me on such short notice. I owe you."

"Yeah, yeah, yeah." Michael hung up and returned the

phone to the center console, then glanced over at Reese. "We have to make a detour to the airport to pick up my mother."

She looked stricken. "You're taking me with you?"

"I don't have time to turn around and drive you back home. We'd never make it to the airport in time. Not in this traffic."

Biting her lip, she glanced down at her snug T-shirt, denim capri pants and pink flip-flops.

Interpreting her thoughts, Michael said impatiently, "Relax. You look fine. And even if you didn't, so what? It's not like you're being introduced as her future daughter-in-law."

Reese bristled. "You should be so lucky."

"What the hell's that supposed to mean?"

"I'll let *you* figure it out." Fuming, she turned away to glare out the passenger window, adding under her breath, "Jerk."

Michael scowled.

So much for their truce.

Chapter 9

Celeste Rutherford was a typical mother in that every time she came for a visit, she reacted as though it had been years since she'd last seen her children, when in her case it had only been four months. She'd flown to Atlanta earlier that year to spend Easter with the family, and before that she'd stayed for two weeks following Christmas. She would have remained longer if her husband—after enduring one too many winter nights alone—hadn't begged her to return home to Minnesota.

When Michael saw his mother standing alone in the bustling airport terminal, he wondered if she'd left Grant behind again. At the sight of Michael, she beamed with such radiant joy that he couldn't help asking himself how he'd ever doubted her love for him.

"Darling!" she cried warmly, rushing forward and wrapping him in one of those rib-crushing embraces that belied her slender, petite frame.

Michael smiled, holding her close. "Hey, Mom. How are you?"

"Couldn't be better, now that you're here." She clung a moment longer, then drew back and cradled his face between her hands, her cinnamon-brown eyes shining with tender adoration. "I swear you get handsomer every time I see you. How is that even possible?"

"I don't know." Michael grinned crookedly. "Are you still refusing to wear your bifocals?"

She laughed, lovingly stroking his cheek. "You look just like your father. It's like stepping back in time."

Michael smiled. "And speaking of that, you look really good, Mom. All your friends must hate you."

"Oh, go on with you, boy," she guffawed, blushing prettily.

At sixty-five, Celeste's smooth café-au-lait skin glowed with an age-defying health and vitality. Her hair was liberally woven with silver and cropped in short, sleek layers that accentuated the serene beauty of her face. Since becoming a frequent flyer in recent years, she'd learned to dress for comfort rather than style, though she still managed to epitomize casual elegance in a breezy summer top, pleated linen slacks and jeweled sandals.

Michael glanced around curiously. "Where's Grant?"

"In the restroom. He'll be right out." Celeste's gaze suddenly landed on Reese, who'd hung back a little to give mother and son privacy. With a discreet glance at Reese's hourglass body poured into snug denim, Celeste undoubtedly reached the conclusion that she was one of her son's latest conquests.

"Hello," Celeste murmured politely.

Michael turned as Reese stepped shyly forward. "Mom, I'd like you to meet Reese St. James. Reese, this is my mother, Celeste Rutherford."

Celeste offered a friendly, if not distant, smile. "How nice to meet you, Reese."

"It's a pleasure to meet you, Mrs. Rutherford," Reese said warmly. "Did you have a good flight?"

Celeste looked pleasantly surprised, as if she hadn't expected Reese to sound so gracious or articulate. *Damn,*

Michael thought with a pang of irritation. *What kind of women does she think I date? I'm not Quentin!*

"Yes, I did enjoy the flight," Celeste answered smoothly. "Thank you for asking, Reese."

Noting the speculative gleam in his mother's eyes, Michael hastened to explain. "Reese just won my apprentice contest."

"Oh! Congratulations!" Celeste exclaimed, clasping both of Reese's hands between hers. "You must be so excited."

"Ecstatic," Reese enthused. "It's an opportunity of a lifetime. I'm a *huge* fan of your son's."

Celeste beamed with pleasure, completely missing the sardonic glance that passed between Michael and Reese.

"I can't tell you how many friends and coworkers tried to bribe me into putting in a good word with Michael," Celeste confided. "After the contest was announced, you won't believe the number of cards, gifts and baked goods I received. And every time I turned around, someone was dropping by for a surprise 'visit.'" She grinned, shaking her head at Reese. "You're going to be the envy of *a lot* of heartbroken women."

Reese sighed dramatically. "Better them than me, I suppose."

Celeste laughed, amused and delighted.

Michael had never been more relieved to see his stepfather approaching. Grant Rutherford was of medium height and build, with a receding thatch of curly gray hair and sharp green eyes that revealed his biracial roots. Dressed in a crisp polo shirt and neatly pressed khaki trousers, he looked like he'd just strolled off his favorite golf course.

He grinned broadly and greeted Michael with a quick bear hug. "Good to see you, Michael. Your mother has been looking forward to this trip ever since she returned from the last one."

Michael smiled. "I'm glad you both could make it." Turning to Reese at his side, he quickly performed the introductions. As Reese shook Grant's hand, she said, "You wouldn't happen to be Dr. Grant Rutherford of the Mayo Clinic, would you?"

Grant nodded. "That would be me."

Reese's face lit up with excitement. "Oh my goodness! It's such an honor to meet you, Dr. Rutherford. I've been following your studies on stem cell research in the *New England Journal of Medicine*."

"Is that right?" Grant beamed, his chest swelling with pride as he eyed her with keen interest. "Young lady, are you a physician?"

Reese nodded. "Obstetrics and gynecology. I work at The Methodist Hospital in Houston."

"You don't say?" Grant's brows arched with obvious approval. "Methodist is a very good facility. I understand it was recently recognized as one of the nation's best hospitals by *U.S. News & World Report*."

Reese grinned. "Yes, sir. We're very proud of that accomplishment."

"As you should be. Where did you go to medical school, Reese?"

"Johns Hopkins."

Grant and Celeste traded looks of such unconcealed delight, you'd have thought Reese had just announced she'd found the cure for cancer.

As they left the busy airport terminal and headed toward the parking garage, Grant and Reese talked shop while Celeste fell in step beside Michael, slipping her arm companionably through his.

"Reese seems like such a wonderful young woman," she gushed. "It looks like you really struck gold with your apprentice search."

Michael did a mental eye roll, wondering if there was *anyone* Reese couldn't charm and impress. His only hope was Sterling, who'd hated practically every woman Michael had ever dated. Though he'd never admit it to the old man, Michael had always valued his father's opinion above anyone else's. Not only did Sterling genuinely have his best interests at heart, but after thirty years as a homicide detective, he'd acquired an uncanny ability to read people. He knew bullshit when he smelled it, and he never hesitated to call a spade a spade.

If anyone could resist Reese's charms, Sterling Wolf could.

Michael only wished he could say the same for himself.

Reclining in the luxurious backseat of the Maybach with Celeste Rutherford, Reese fielded questions about work, her family and growing up in Houston. She asked Grant Rutherford about his latest clinical research study and chatted about everything from the weather to the bad economy. But if asked later to recall specific details of the conversation, she would have been at a complete loss.

She'd been unable to concentrate on anything since arguing with Michael that morning. She was still reeling with shock, anger and confusion over the way he'd lashed out at her for having a boyfriend. He'd reacted like a scorned lover. Which was absurd, considering that he and Reese had hated each other's guts just yesterday. If *she* hadn't shown up at his penthouse seeking a truce, they'd still be bitter enemies today. He had no right to be jealous of her relationship with another man.

But he *had* been jealous, and that realization left her shaken and more conflicted than ever.

When she'd received a call that morning from a local florist notifying her that a driver was en route to her house, Reese had known right away that Victor had sent her roses. Exasperated by his stubborn persistence, she'd thanked the florist and called Victor, intending to give him another earful about not respecting her boundaries. But he'd masterfully deflected her ire, and by the time the doorbell rang, he'd had Reese laughing and reminiscing about the first time they'd ever met. Before the conversation ended he'd told her that he loved her and missed her, but he was willing to give her the space she'd asked for.

And then Michael had arrived—and all hell broke loose.

If Reese were being honest with herself, she would admit that Michael wasn't entirely in the wrong. The truth was that she'd been giving him mixed signals ever since they'd met. First she'd asked him to drive her home with the intent of seducing him, then she'd spent an entire day with him, laughing and bonding with him. From Michael's perspective, she was acting like a tease, saying one thing and doing another. It wasn't fair to him, and it sure as hell wasn't fair to Victor.

So it had to stop, Reese vowed.

No matter how powerful the attraction between her and Michael, she had to resist temptation and keep their relationship strictly platonic. It was the only way she'd get through the next two months with her integrity—and sanity—intact.

But when she glanced up and caught Michael's dark gaze in the rearview mirror, instant heat swamped her body.

Swallowing hard, she jerked her eyes away and smiled brightly at his mother.

No one ever said resisting temptation was easy.

Thirty minutes later, Reese found herself leaning toward the window as the car glided down a winding country road flanked by huge magnolia trees. She stared, riveted by the sight of a sprawling redbrick house that boasted tall windows overlooking riotously blooming flowers.

Michael turned into the driveway, passing an expanse of manicured lawn and a small lake in the center of the property before he came to a stop behind a silver Buick.

"Wow." The single word escaped Reese in a hushed whisper.

Beside her, Celeste Rutherford smiled. "Amazing, isn't it? Michael and his brother bought this house for their father several years ago. The first time I came here, I was simply blown away. Wait until you see the backyard. The garden will leave you breathless."

They climbed out of the car, and while Michael and Grant retrieved the luggage from the trunk, the two women started toward the house. They were met at the front door by a middle-aged woman who introduced herself to Reese as Frizell Randolph, Sterling's personal chef.

"Where's Sterling?" Celeste asked the woman as they entered the house.

"He's in the backyard with Ms. Dubois. Last I checked, they were discussing seating arrangements for the reception dinner. Samara just left to pick up the twins from day care. She promised to hurry back as soon as she can, along with Marcus."

Reese glanced around the house, taking in the double-height foyer, butterfly staircases and chandelier lifts. Thick Aubusson rugs were spread across glossy hardwood floors, and fresh-cut flowers were arranged in crystal vases on gleaming mahogany tables.

"Let me show you the backyard while Michael and Grant carry the bags upstairs," Celeste said, draping an arm companionably around Reese's shoulders.

As they started from the foyer, Grant could be overheard grumbling to Michael, "I don't know why your mother insisted on packing so much clothes. We're only staying for two weeks."

Michael chuckled. "Or so you think."

Celeste ushered Reese through the house to a pair of double French doors that opened onto an enormous veranda. As they stepped outside and crossed to the railing, Reese saw that Celeste had not exaggerated about the backyard, which was huge and nothing short of breathtaking.

But before she could take it all in, her attention was diverted by a burst of loud, angry voices. Celeste muttered under her breath as a man and a woman suddenly emerged from a dense thicket of trees and began marching toward the house.

Reese stared in incredulous disbelief. What shocked her

wasn't the sight of two grown adults squabbling like children on a playground. Rather, it was the sight of the tall, dark-skinned man who bore such a striking resemblance to Michael that Reese wondered whether she'd unwittingly stumbled into a time warp projected twenty years into the future.

Her gaze moved to the woman next. She was tall, voluptuous and stunningly beautiful. Dressed in a stylish white pantsuit and stiletto heels, she strode down the flagstone walkway with the icy hauteur of a seasoned runway model.

As Reese stared at the woman, recognition dawned. Her eyes widened. "Wait a minute. Is that—"

"Asha Dubois," Celeste finished sourly. "Yes, it is."

Judging by her tone and the grim set of her mouth, it was obvious that Celeste was no fan of Asha Dubois, a world-renowned fashion designer who was in town to celebrate the grand opening of her Lenox Square boutique—an event that was garnering as much buzz on local radio stations as Michael's return home the week before. In her youth, Asha had been a supermodel whose exotic beauty had graced countless magazine covers. After retiring from the runway, she'd gone on to successfully launch her own clothing empire, becoming one of the first African-American designers to conquer the cutthroat world of haute couture.

Reese, whose own closet was filled with House of Dubois fashions, couldn't help feeling a little starstruck at the prospect of meeting Asha Dubois. Though barely fifty, the woman was already a living legend.

"My son Marcus is married to her daughter," Celeste volunteered.

"Really?" Reese silently marveled at the odds of her meeting a celebrity chef, a prominent neurosurgeon and a famous fashion designer in less than a week. And—astonishingly—they were all in the same extended family.

As Sterling Wolf and Asha Dubois drew nearer to the house, Reese couldn't help noticing what a striking pair they made. But based on the way they were quarreling with each other, it was abundantly clear there was no love lost between them.

"...I don't even know why I bothered to consult with you," Asha was venting. Even in her anger, her voice was cool and cultured. "You don't know the first thing about hosting a classy affair. My God, if it were up to you, we would have served pork ribs and beans at our children's wedding reception!"

"And what the hell's wrong with that?" Sterling fired back. "In case you haven't noticed, woman, we're in the South. And we Southerners happen to enjoy our barbecue!"

Asha shuddered. "Not at a wedding."

"*Even* at a wedding!" He snorted derisively. "Hell, if you weren't such a stuck up witch—"

Asha glared at him. "Who're you calling a witch, you old—"

Celeste cleared her throat loudly, and the two combatants looked around in surprise. When they saw Celeste and Reese watching them from the railing, their expressions turned sheepish.

"We have company," Celeste announced sweetly.

"So I see." Sterling Wolf stepped onto the veranda, his dark eyes homing in on Reese. "Well, hello there. And who might you be?"

Reese smiled, suddenly nervous about coming face-to-face with Michael's father. He cut an imposing figure with his neatly trimmed salt-and-pepper hair, keenly intelligent gaze and tall, robust build.

Seeing that Reese was momentarily tongue-tied, Celeste came to her rescue. "Sterling, this is Reese St. James, Michael's new apprentice."

Sterling's heavy brows shot up, and a wide grin swept across his ruggedly handsome face. "It's a pleasure to make your acquaintance, Miss St. James," he said, his large, callused hand enveloping hers in a firm handshake. "Welcome to Atlanta."

Reese smiled shyly. "Thank you, Mr. Wolf. You have a beautiful home."

"Thank you kindly. I've learned to appreciate it." His eyes twinkled, giving her a glimpse of the devilish charm that obviously flowed in the Wolf gene pool.

"Reese is a doctor," Celeste told him proudly.

"So I've heard." Sterling smiled, leaving Reese to wonder what else he knew about her. "Will you be joining us for dinner this evening?"

Before Reese could respond, an amused voice drawled, "Doesn't waste any time, does he?"

Both Celeste and Sterling turned to glare at Asha, who sat at a white wrought-iron table idly sipping from a glass of wine that had materialized out of nowhere. Her long, shapely legs were crossed, and her black hair was slicked back into an elegant chignon that accentuated her high cheekbones, sultry dark eyes and lush, sensual mouth.

"Asha," Celeste murmured, forcing a smile that looked as if she had a lip full of Novocain. "You're looking well."

Asha inclined her head. *"Merci."* She didn't return the compliment—deliberately, Reese suspected.

Before Celeste could even register the slight, Asha's eyes traveled to Reese's face, giving her a swift, evaluative once-over. "You have excellent bone structure. Please tell me you've done some modeling before."

"No, ma'am. I haven't." Reese smiled, not immune to receiving such a compliment from the legendary fashion designer.

Asha shook her head. "What a shame."

"Maybe." Reese shrugged. "But even if I wanted to model, I'm too old to do anything about it now."

Asha gave a low, indulgent laugh. "A word of advice, darling. Never admit to being too old for anything. Isn't that right, Celeste?"

Celeste bristled, her face reddening at the veiled insult.

Sterling leveled a narrow glance at Asha. "Woman, don't you have places to go? People to see?"

"Not at the moment," she said blandly. "Besides, after running around with Samara all morning, I need a break from this suffocating heat. I don't know how you people can stand it."

"No one told you to schedule your grand opening at the height of summer," Celeste snidely pointed out.

"True enough." Asha took a languid sip of wine. "And no one told *you* to move to the frozen tundra of Minnesota. But I suppose your personality is better suited to frigid weather."

Celeste sputtered with indignation. "How dare—"

Sterling laid a gentle, restraining hand upon her arm. "We have company, remember?"

She darted a glance at Reese then clamped her jaw shut, seething with suppressed fury as she glared at Asha.

Sterling gave Reese a conciliatory smile. "You have to excuse us old folks. We get cranky when we haven't had our nap."

"Speak for yourself." Asha sipped more wine, her gaze returning to Reese. "Have you been invited to my reception on Monday?"

"Um, no, I—"

"Then consider this your invitation." Asha looked at Sterling. "You don't mind, do you? When Michael told me you'd agreed to let me use your home to host the event, he gave me free rein to invite as many people as I wanted."

"I don't mind at all." Sterling smiled tightly at Reese. "I would have invited you myself if she hadn't beat me to it."

"Who beat you to what?"

Four pairs of eyes swung around to find Michael standing at the entrance to the veranda. He took one look at his parents' strained faces, then Asha's smug expression, and slowly shook his head.

"Never mind," he muttered. "I don't want to know."

Reese couldn't help noticing the way he'd deliberately avoided looking at her. *Fine,* she thought crossly. *If he wants to pretend I'm invisible, two can play that game!*

"Hello, Michael," Asha murmured. "I was just beginning to wonder if you'd ever show up."

"Asha." Michael bent to kiss her upturned cheek. "It's good to see you again. Ready for next Monday?"

"I'm *always* ready." She smiled. "Darling, I hope you'll forgive me for scheduling my grand opening on the same day as your show's season premiere. I didn't realize the dates coincided until it was too late. You know the last thing I want to do is steal your spotlight."

"Like hell," Celeste muttered under her breath.

Ignoring his mother, Michael said smoothly, "Don't worry about it, Asha. We always tape the show in the morning, so there won't be a conflict with your reception that evening. And the studio usually throws a small party to celebrate the season premiere, so either way, I'm gonna have a good time that night."

"Wonderful." Asha beamed with pleasure. "If you have some time, Michael, I thought we could go over the reception menu and seating arrangements, maybe take another tour of the garden to finalize the layout."

"Absolutely," he agreed. "We can meet now, if you'd like."

"Absolutely." Asha uncrossed her legs and glided to her feet with a sensual, feline grace that would make any man drool.

"I'm dying to see how your staff will decorate the garden," Asha told Michael. "They did such a fabulous job for Marcus and Samara's wedding. It's hard to imagine them topping themselves."

Michael flashed a grin. "Then you're in for a real treat. I met with them on Saturday, and I think you'll be very pleased with what they have in mind."

"I don't doubt it," Asha said with a lazy smile.

Reese silently berated herself for feeling a sharp stab of jealousy when Asha linked her arm through Michael's.

"Michael," Celeste said tightly, "where's Grant?"

"He had to make a few phone calls. Sorry—I meant to tell you when I first came out."

"That's okay. You were obviously distracted." Shooting

one last withering look at Asha, Celeste muttered an excuse about having a headache and stalked back into the house.

Michael cocked a brow at his father. "Did I miss something?"

Chuckling drily, Sterling waved him off. "Go on with Asha. Reese and I are gonna sit out here, sip lemonade and get better acquainted. I hope that's okay with you, Reese?"

She gave him her sunniest smile. "I'd like that very much."

Michael looked from one to the other, eyes narrowed. "We won't be long," he said curtly, and strode off with Asha.

Chapter 10

Michael was still in a foul mood that evening.

Nursing his second glass of Merlot, he cast a surly glance around the long mahogany dinner table, which had been set with Sterling's best china and decorated with fresh flowers from the garden. Ms. Frizell, with minor input from Michael, had prepared a lavish five-course feast fit for royalty.

Everyone seemed to be having a good time. Presiding at the head of the table, Sterling engaged Grant in a spirited debate about the best golf courses in Georgia versus Minnesota. Marcus and Samara had their hands full with the twins, alternately cajoling the boys to eat their vegetables and laughing at their antics. Even Celeste and Asha were being civil to each other, honoring their unspoken agreement never to argue in front of their grandchildren.

And then there was Reese.

Reese, whose radiant smiles and engaging personality made it impossible for anyone to treat her as an outsider. In brooding resignation, Michael watched her work her charm on his family, laughing and bantering with that natural ease he'd grown to admire. Even his nephews fell under her spell, giggling at the goofy faces she made at them and vying for her attention.

Michael couldn't take his eyes off her. In contrast, Reese had barely spared him a glance all evening.

Earlier, he'd returned from meeting with Asha to find Reese and his father right where he'd left them on the veranda, sipping lemonade and sharing a laugh like old friends. Michael had known the verdict even before Sterling met his gaze and mouthed: *She's a keeper, Mike.*

Those four unforgettable words, never before uttered by his father, had plunged Michael into an even blacker mood—a volatile cocktail of anger, frustration and longing. And the more Reese ignored him over dinner, the worse his mood became.

After dinner, everyone gravitated to the backyard as dusk approached. While the others roamed the landscaped grounds, Michael stayed on the veranda seated at a table under the pretext of making some phone calls. He checked his voice mail messages, then dialed the restaurant to see how things were going. After speaking to his sous chef for a few minutes, he hung up just as he received a text message from Lexi.

How's the family visit going? she wrote. *Is the diva still breathing?*

Michael couldn't suppress a wry chuckle. Lexi knew all about his parents' acrimonious relationship with Asha Dubois. She'd often had Michael in stitches as she concocted slapstick scenarios in which Sterling and Celeste plotted to get rid of Asha, only to be thwarted at every turn by the "diva who wouldn't die."

Smiling, Michael typed back, *The diva's alive and well. And fine as hell.*

A moment later Lexi responded. *You sound just like Q.*

Michael scowled. *Low blow,* he shot back.

Sorry, came her amused reply. *Couldn't resist. Anyway, some friends and I are meeting Q for drinks. Wanna come? You can keep your boy in line.*

An Important Message from the Publisher

Dear Reader,

Because you've chosen to read one of our fine novels, I'd like to say "thank you"! And, as a special way to say thank you, I'm offering to send you two more Kimani™ Romance novels and two surprise gifts – absolutely FREE! These books will keep it real with true-to-life African American characters that turn up the heat and sizzle with passion.

Please enjoy the free books and gifts with our compliments...

Glenda Howard

For Kimani Press

Peel off Seal and Place Inside...

Michael paused, his gaze straying to where Reese was playing hide-and-seek with the twins. The boys were giggling hysterically, their short, sturdy legs pumping as they tried to evade capture, a task made easy by Reese's exaggeratedly slow running.

Michael watched them, his chest squeezing as he envisioned Reese pregnant. Holding his baby in her arms. Chasing *their* child around the yard.

Shaken by the images, he jerked his gaze back to the phone, where Lexi was awaiting his response to her invitation. He wondered what she would say if she knew about his growing feelings for Reese, the very same woman he'd vehemently objected to having on his show just three days ago. He'd always sought Lexi's advice about women, but for some reason he didn't want to tell her about Reese. His feelings for her were too new, too confusing, too powerful.

Too damn scary.

Are you there? Lexi prompted.

Michael cleared his throat and quickly typed, *Can't meet for drinks. But how about lunch on Thursday?*

Your treat?

Of course.

Then you're on, baby.

Michael grinned. *Have fun tonight and tell Q to behave, or else….*

He sent the message, then stuffed his phone into the back pocket of his jeans.

As his brooding gaze wandered back to Reese, Marcus climbed onto the veranda and cautiously approached, eyeing Michael as if he were a feral animal who might pounce at any moment.

When Marcus had nearly reached the table, he stopped and asked, "Is it safe to proceed?"

Michael just looked at him.

"Remember when we were younger, and I'd take stuff from your room and forget to put it back before you noticed it was missing? Remember when I was six and I accidentally tore your autographed Dominique Wilkins poster? Well, the way you're looking at me now is the way you looked at me that day. Man, I was so scared you'd beat the crap out of me that I peed on myself. Remember that?"

Michael tried, but couldn't stifle his laughter.

Marcus grinned, looking relieved as he pulled out a chair at the table and nimbly straddled it. "Dad was so mad that I'd ruined a new pair of pants that he whipped my butt, anyway."

"Believe it or not, little man, you got off lucky that day. I was mad enough to strangle you. I *loved* that poster."

"I know. But at least I made it up to you."

"Yeah, you did," Michael agreed, thinking of the way Marcus had invited the NBA legend to his fortieth birthday bash. Michael's gift from Dominique Wilkins, of course, had been an autographed poster to replace the one Marcus had ripped years ago.

Michael smiled at the memory, feeling some of the tension ebb from his body.

It didn't last.

"So what's up with you and Reese?" Marcus demanded, dropping all pretenses of making small talk.

Michael frowned. "Nothing's up with us."

"Like hell," Marcus snorted. "You've been sulking all night, and she's been going out of her way to treat you like the Invisible Man. What the hell happened between you two?"

"I don't wanna talk about it," Michael bit off.

Undaunted, Marcus pressed, "What changed between yesterday morning and today? Q says you and Reese looked mighty cozy together when he saw you at the restaurant."

Michael glared at his brother. "He told you about that?"

Marcus gave him a *come-on-now* look.

Michael swore under his breath. Of course Quentin had run his mouth to Marcus. He always did.

"On second thought," Michael groused, "maybe it *wasn't* such a good idea for you to hire Q. The two of you have way too much time on your hands at the office."

Marcus smiled. "Actually, I think we're pretty productive. And you haven't answered my question. How did you and Reese go from being lovey-dovey to not even speaking to each other?"

Scowling, Michael shoved to his feet and stalked over to the railing. Striving for calm, he stared out across the sprawling yard, mentally cataloguing the idyllic scene before him. His mother and Grant lounged in the gazebo, while Sterling and Asha strolled along the walkway swinging their grandsons between them. Reese and Samara now sat talking by the small pool, their bare legs dangling in the shimmering water.

As Michael watched Reese, a deep ache of longing washed through him. He recognized it as the same feeling he'd experienced at Marcus's wedding, a feeling that had resurfaced in recent days.

The day after he met Reese, to be exact.

Marcus joined him at the railing. Following the direction of his brother's gaze, he smiled. "Those two look like they've been friends for years."

Michael grunted in agreement.

Marcus sighed. "I've always hoped that when—and if—you ever get married, our wives will be as close as we are."

Michael slanted his brother a look that would have sent a lesser man scurrying under the table. But Marcus merely grinned.

"Don't go planning any weddings just yet," Michael grumbled. "Reese has a boyfriend."

"Ahh." Marcus nodded wisely. "That explains the tortured expression on your face every time you look at her."

"I don't have a 'tortured' expression." But even as the swift denial left Michael's mouth, it rang hollow in his ears.

Marcus gave him an almost pitying look. "I can definitely see how you got blindsided. Reese is a beautiful woman. Smart as hell, too." He chuckled. "Mom can't stop mentioning that she's a doctor."

"Yeah," Michael said, his mouth twisting cynically, "and we all know how Mom feels about doctors."

It was an ugly thing to say, a barbed reference to the way Celéste had deserted them in favor of Grant Rutherford, the rich, handsome surgeon at the hospital where she'd worked. For years Michael had despised doctors so much that he couldn't even watch them on TV. And now here he was making a fool of himself over, of all things, a doctor. Oh, the irony.

"So, what're you gonna do about it?" Marcus asked, resting his arms on the railing.

"Do about what?"

"Your feelings for Reese. What're you gonna do about it?"

Michael frowned at his brother. "Didn't you hear what I just said? She has a boyfriend."

"Is it serious?"

"How the hell should I know?" Michael snapped. He didn't *want* to know. The thought of Reese with another man made him feel downright homicidal.

"So that's it, then. Because she's already in a relationship, you're backing off. Just like that."

"Damn straight."

Marcus nodded thoughtfully. "Interestingly enough, I didn't see a ring on any of her fingers."

"Doesn't matter. You know my rule."

"Right. The rule." Marcus's tone was faintly mocking. "You know what they say about rules, don't you?"

"What?"

"There's always an exception."

That shut Michael up. He faltered for a moment, then blew out a harsh, exasperated breath. He could feel a vein throbbing in his neck and he flexed his fingers, fighting a vicious urge to punch Marcus in the mouth. Michael loved his brother to death and would do anything for him, but ever since he'd gotten married, Marcus had become *way* too interested in Michael's love life. It was as if he'd made it his personal mission to get Michael hitched so that he'd be as deliriously happy as *he* was.

Marcus released a dramatic sigh. "If you're not interested

in going after what you want, Q says he'd be more than happy—"

"Like hell he will," Michael growled, skewering Marcus with a lethal glare. "If Q goes anywhere near Reese, you're gonna have one less lawyer on your damn payroll. Get what I'm saying?"

Marcus chuckled, edging slightly away from him. "Loud and clear."

Michael clenched his jaw, his nerves stretched dangerously taut.

After a prolonged silence, Marcus said offhandedly, "Samara and I are gonna crash here for the night. Why don't you and Reese do the same? You know Dad's got plenty of room, and quite frankly, you don't look like you should be getting behind the wheel tonight."

Michael bristled. "I only had two glasses of wine with dinner."

Marcus grinned. "Your alcohol intake isn't what I'm worried about. Given your rotten mood, do you really think it's a good idea for you to be alone in a car with Reese?"

Before Michael could respond, a high-pitched squeal from one of the twins drew his gaze across the yard to Sterling and Asha. As he and Marcus watched, their father tossed Matt into the air and caught him with a deep, rollicking laugh. Balancing Malcolm on one hip, Asha laughingly admonished Sterling to be careful. Instead of scowling or flagging her off, Sterling smiled and brushed a windblown strand of hair off her face.

Michael and Marcus exchanged startled glances.

"Did you see that?" Marcus asked.

"Hell, yeah."

They watched in disbelief as Asha smiled shyly at their father before averting her eyes to kiss Malcolm's forehead. Sterling gazed at her a moment longer, then blinked and quickly glanced away.

Michael gave his brother a sideways look. "You don't think...?"

They went still, staring alertly at each other.

"Nah," they scoffed in unison, and laughed.

Chapter 11

Around midnight, Reese found herself wide awake and staring up at a dark ceiling. Despite being enveloped in Egyptian cotton sheets, and despite the fact that she'd drank three glasses of wine over dinner, sleep eluded her.

And she knew the reason.

She was spending the night under the same roof as Michael. The knowledge that he was asleep somewhere in this big house had proved to be too much for her overactive imagination. Every time she closed her eyes, her mind conjured an image of his hard, muscular, *naked* body sprawled across a bed. A bed that was calling her name.

It was no wonder her throat was parched and her body burned with a fever that had nothing to do with the sweltering temperature outside.

With a muffled groan of frustration, she flung back the covers and slid out of bed. What she needed was a tall glass of water and maybe some fresh air to clear her head.

Before leaving the guest bedroom, she finger-combed her tousled hair just in case she ran into anyone downstairs.

Glancing down at herself, she surveyed the silk nightshirt Samara Wolf had loaned to her before bedtime. Samara was an inch or two taller, so the nightshirt caught Reese just below the knee. Though she would have preferred the added layer of a robe, she figured she looked decent enough to venture out.

Crossing to the door, she crept from the room and started down the wide corridor. Her footfalls were absorbed by the thick Aubusson rug that ran the length of the floor.

As she passed the bedroom shared by Marcus and Samara, she thought she heard soft sighs and moans coming from within. She grinned to herself, remembering the intimate looks the couple had exchanged throughout the evening. Despite having their hands full with two rambunctious toddlers, it was clear that their passion for each other had not abated.

Reese hoped that she and her future husband—if she ever got married—would share that same kind of sexual chemistry, the kind that stood the test of time.

Descending the curved staircase, she headed toward the kitchen. The house was dark and silent. Thankfully, it appeared that she was the only insomniac wandering around late at night.

Her steps slowed as she neared the double French doors that led to the veranda. Moonlight poured in through the tall windows and washed over her. As if drawn by some invisible force, she drifted forward and gazed out into the dark, starry night. There was a full moon, and she could feel the sultry nocturnal heat pressing against the glass. Heedless, she reached for the doorknob and slowly eased the door open, praying she wouldn't trigger a security alarm that would awaken the entire household.

When no alarm sounded, she breathed a sigh of relief and stepped outside, quietly pulling the door closed behind her. The wood was smooth and warm beneath her bare feet as she padded across the veranda to reach the railing. She closed her eyes, inhaling the fragrant mélange of roses, azaleas, hydrangeas and night-blooming jasmine from the garden below. Already she could feel some of the tension melting from her body.

"Couldn't sleep?"

Reese gasped and whirled around, heart lodged in her throat.

At the sight of Michael sitting alone in a shadowy corner of the veranda, her knees went weak and she sagged against the railing. "You scared me half to death! Are you trying to give me a heart attack?"

"Not quite." His voice was a deep, smoky rumble in the dark night. Heat curled through her veins, fueling the restless ache between her thighs.

She swallowed, straightening from the balustrade. "W-what're you doing sitting out here in the dark? Howling at the moon?" she joked lamely.

She thought she detected the ghost of a smile on his face. As she stared at him, he tipped back his head and howled ever so softly. She shivered with arousal, her nipples hardening and her clitoris swelling.

Silently cursing her body's reaction to him, she cleared her throat and shifted from one foot to another. "I, uh, hope I'm not disturbing you."

"You are," came his lazy drawl, "but what else is new?"

Unnerved, Reese made a move toward the house. "In that case, I'll just—"

"Stay," Michael said, a low, husky command.

She obeyed without question.

"Why couldn't you sleep?" he asked her.

"Who says I couldn't sleep?" she retorted defiantly.

"You're out here, aren't you?"

She shrugged, feigning nonchalance. "Maybe I just wanted some fresh air."

"So you roused yourself from a deep sleep just to come outside—where it's ninety-five degrees—and get some fresh air." His voice was heavy with amused skepticism.

Reese said nothing. She was glad he couldn't see the deep flush suffusing her cheeks.

"Wanna know what I think?" he asked softly.

She swallowed. "Not particularly."

"I think you're out here for the same reason I am."

Her pulse hammered at the base of her throat as he stood and came toward her, a slow, deliberate advance. She felt a frisson of fear mingled with excitement.

Resisting the urge to bolt, she held her ground as he stopped just inches from her. She could feel the heat radiating from his big body, could smell a lingering trace of his cologne underlaid by warm male skin. Her mouth watered, and it was all she could do not to pounce on him and tear off his clothes.

His gaze raked over her, taking in her silk nightshirt and bare feet in one hot, encompassing sweep. His eyes glittered like a wolf's in the moonlight.

"I think you couldn't sleep because you were thinking about me," he said in that sinfully intoxicating voice. "I know, because I was thinking about *you*, imagining you warm and naked between the sheets, your body calling out for mine. I got so damn hard that I couldn't take it anymore. If I hadn't gotten out of the house when I did, you would've found me in your bed."

Oh God, Reese thought as a rush of liquid heat bloomed between her thighs. She started to sway toward him before she caught herself and stepped backward, holding up a hand as if to ward him off. "Michael—"

"Tell me you weren't thinking about me," he taunted, daring her.

"I wasn't thinking about you."

"Liar."

They faced each other in the moonlit darkness, the air between them vibrating with a potent combination of tension, frustration, anger and lust.

Needing to put some distance between them, Reese sidestepped Michael and strode to the other end of the veranda, relieved when he let her go. Impulsively she grabbed the beer bottle he'd been nursing, shook it, then raised it to her mouth and downed the rest of the contents.

When she'd finished, she slammed the bottle down on the table with a metallic thud.

"Feel better?" Michael murmured, faintly amused.

"No," she snapped, keeping her back to him. "Truth be told, I probably won't 'feel better' until I'm back home in Texas." *Safely far away from you!*

"Are you homesick, Reese?" His voice was deceptively mild.

She hesitated. He'd misinterpreted her words, but instead of telling him that, she said, "Yes, as a matter of fact, I *am* feeling a little homesick." As soon as the ridiculous lie left her mouth, she instinctively knew he'd make her pay for it.

She heard a whisper of movement behind her.

And then suddenly he was right there, reaching her with a predatory stealth that made her wonder if he really was a wolf in disguise.

She let out a startled cry as he seized her, hauling her against him, bringing her backside into electrifying contact with his thick, rigid arousal. Desire exploded in her veins. Her heart thundered furiously.

He surrounded her, scorching her with his heat and virile intensity. "Reese," he whispered, hoarse with need and longing as he tenderly stroked her hair and brushed his lips across her temple. "Beautiful, *beautiful,* Reese. What are you doing to me?"

Disarmed by his unexpected gentleness and the aching vulnerability in his voice, she let her body relax against his. She trembled as his mouth wandered to the edge of her jaw, seeking the corner of her lips. Closing her eyes, she turned her face into his and opened to the exquisite taste of him, powerless to resist. He kissed her as if their bodies were already joined, deep, hungry kisses she felt down in her wet, throbbing loins. The pleasure was so intense it was almost unbearable.

Suddenly his hands were everywhere on her body, stoking the flames inside her. When he cupped her bottom, she moaned and gyrated her hips, grinding against the hot, bulging pressure of his erection. He groaned, low and guttural.

"I want you. Want you so bad it's all I've tasted for days," he whispered raggedly against the curve of her neck. His teeth sank into her tender flesh, sending waves of erotic sensation crashing through her.

She shuddered uncontrollably, her head falling back against his hard chest. Now *she* wanted to howl at the moon.

He bit her gently, rasping his tongue against her hammering pulse while he reached for the hem of her nightshirt and slowly dragged it up her bare thighs. Reese shivered at the cool kiss of silk against her fevered skin. His big, callused hands slid over her belly and past her heaving rib cage before cupping her swollen breasts. She cried out, raw pleasure rippling through her.

"Mmm," he rumbled huskily. "I've dreamed about these every night since we met."

Reese groaned, writhing against him as his fingers teased and stroked her erect nipples, deepening the sweet, pulsing ache in her womb. Her clitoris was engorged, and her panties were completely soaked. She wanted him to drag her down to the floor and take her, any and every way he pleased.

"Please..." she begged, trying desperately to remember why what they were doing was so wrong. "We can't... We shouldn't be doing this."

"Why not?" His voice was rough with leashed fury. "Because of him?"

She swallowed and bobbed her head weakly.

"Well, he's not here," Michael snarled. "*I'm* here. And I'm not going anywhere. So you'd better get damn used to it."

Her heart thumped violently. "Michael—"

He slanted his mouth over hers, silencing her with a fierce, plundering kiss that left her quaking from head to toe.

"Does he want you the way that I do?" he whispered savagely, his hands tightening over her breasts, kneading and caressing them. "Can he sleep? Can he breathe? Can he *think* about anything other than being buried deep inside you?"

Reese moaned as her knees threatened to buckle.

"When he makes love to you," Michael relentlessly demanded, "does he worship your body? Does he know when you want it hard and fast, or when you want to be taken nice and slow? Does he *know* you?"

A pathetic whimper escaped her.

Gripping her by the waist, Michael sank to his haunches behind her. Her pulse thudded, a fine sheen of sweat breaking out on her skin. She licked her lips, dizzy with desire and anticipation as he reached under the nightshirt and grasped the waistband of her panties. The damp scrap of lace rubbed her swollen clitoris as he dragged the underwear down her legs, the friction making her mewl in wanton response.

Trembling, she braced her hands on the table and bowed her head, her hair hanging over her face as he caressed the swell of her bottom, crooning softly in masculine appreciation.

"What about now, Reese? Still feeling homesick?"

His words were taunting, but she heard the unmistakable arousal in his deep voice, felt the coiled tension in his body. He was as close to losing it as she was, and just knowing that whipped her into a near frenzy of lust.

He slipped his hands between her shaking thighs, coaxing them apart. She was so sensitized that the faintest brush of his knuckles almost made her come right then and there.

Slowly, provocatively, he ran his finger down the cleft of her bottom, tormenting her as he inched ever closer to her drenched, pulsing sex. Just when she was on the verge of climbing out of her skin, he parted the slick folds of her labia and slid his long finger inside her. She cried out wildly, arching her back and raising her butt higher against him. His low, rumbling groan of pleasure thrilled and inflamed her.

"You're so wet," he purred in ruthless satisfaction. "You're wet for me, aren't you, Reese? Not him—*me*."

She couldn't think, couldn't speak, her mind and body completely turned over to his will.

As his finger pushed deeper inside her, she let out a shuddering moan and undulated her hips against his hand, craving more of the erotic, gliding friction. He murmured softly in approval and eased another finger inside her, stretching her. A broken sob caught in her throat. Her thighs trembled as he expertly worked her tender flesh. Her inner muscles tightened and clutched around him, straining for release.

And then he pressed his hot mouth to her sex.

A strangled cry erupted from her throat.

She bent low over the table, gripping the edge so hard she broke a nail. He tasted her, stroking his tongue up and down her labia before pulling her clitoris between his lips.

It was too much for her.

She shot to her tiptoes and came with a violent shudder, biting her lip to stifle the keening wail that rose up in her throat. A wail that would have awakened the entire neighborhood.

It was the most earth-shattering orgasm she'd ever had. She rode it out hard, her body convulsing for what seemed an eternity.

It was only when she'd grown still that Michael took his tormenting mouth from her and moved back.

As the fog of lust gradually cleared from her brain and sanity returned, a wave of shame engulfed her. Her newfound resolve to resist temptation hadn't even lasted a day.

When Michael silently held out her lace panties, her cheeks flamed with humiliation. With as much dignity as she could muster, she took her underwear from his hand and turned away to slide them back on. Her hands shook as she pulled down her nightshirt and smoothed it over her thighs.

After taking a deep, steadying breath, she turned to face him.

He had risen to his feet. He seemed even taller as he towered over her, though she didn't know whether it was a trick of the moonlight or a perception contrived by her shattered nerves.

She swallowed hard, resisting the urge to step backward in cowardly retreat. Squaring her shoulders, she said evenly, "Look, I understand what just happened here. After the way

I ignored you tonight, you wanted to prove to both of us that I'm still attracted to you. Fine. Mission accomplished. But that doesn't change anything between us, Michael. As you confirmed today, I *am* in a relationship, and until that changes, you and I have to keep our hands—and mouths—off each other. Deal?"

A shadow of a smile curved his lips, and he shook his head slowly at her. "You don't understand, sweetheart."

She sighed impatiently. "Don't call me—"

"That was just an appetizer," he continued huskily, his dark eyes glittering with illicit promise. "It's only a matter of time before I'll have you for the main course."

Reese's stomach bottomed out.

They stared at each other for a long, electrified moment.

And then, without another word, she turned and fled back into the house like the coward she was.

Sterling Wolf considered himself the luckiest man in the world.

He had his health, he lived in a beautiful house that was the envy of his neighbors and he enjoyed more of an active social life than many men half his age. But what Sterling was most grateful for, what he treasured most in the entire world, was his family. Not only had he been blessed with two of the best sons any father could ever ask for, but he now had a wonderful daughter-in-law and two grandchildren he absolutely adored. The Lord had blessed him indeed.

So he didn't need a woman by his side to make him feel complete. After the way his marriage had ended nearly thirty years ago, Sterling figured he was better off alone, anyway. Not that he lacked for female companionship. Even a man his age still had needs, and he indulged them discreetly whenever possible. But in the years since his divorce, no woman had ever made him consider taking another stab at marriage.

Until today.

The strangest thing had happened while he and Asha were

playing with their grandsons that evening. One moment he'd been tossing Matt into the air; the next moment he was staring into Asha's laughing eyes and feeling like he'd been sucker punched in the gut. And Asha—who oozed more sex appeal than any woman he'd ever known—had given him the shy smile of a virgin on her wedding night.

Hours later, Sterling was still scratching his head, trying to make sense of that odd little exchange. It was no secret to anyone that he and Asha detested each other, to the extent that if Sterling ever *did* find himself in the market for a wife, Asha would be the *last* person on earth he'd ever consider marrying. She was bourgeois, selfish, manipulative and too damn used to getting her own way. Her world revolved around hosting ritzy fashion shows, running her clothing empire and jet-setting to Paris at the drop of a dime, while the highlight of Sterling's social calendar was the annual fishing trip he took with his retired police buddies. Asha liked champagne and caviar, while Sterling couldn't fathom why any sane person would willingly eat fish eggs.

They were as opposite as any two people could be, and had absolutely nothing in common.

With one exception. They both doted shamelessly on their grandsons.

While Asha would be the first to admit that she'd been a lousy mother to Samara, no one could dispute what an excellent grandmother she was. The boys couldn't ask for a more loving, attentive grandma.

So it shouldn't have surprised Sterling to find Asha sitting quietly in a corner when he crept into the twins' bedroom late that night.

Matthew and Malcolm had been born premature, requiring a monthlong hospital stay that had put everyone—especially Marcus and Samara—through the wringer. Though both boys were now as strong and healthy as could be, Sterling had taken to checking up on them in the middle of the night whenever they came for a visit.

Apparently he wasn't the only one.

The tender expression on Asha's face as she gazed upon their sleeping grandsons made something tighten in Sterling's chest.

When she glanced up and their eyes met, a strange current of awareness passed between them.

He froze, staring at her in the warm glow of the lightning-bug night-light. She sat in the big rocking chair Sterling had bought for the nursery after the twins were born. She wore a silk kimono and matching slippers, and her thick black hair fell in soft disarray about her shoulders. With her face scrubbed clean of expensive cosmetics, she looked even younger than usual. Softer, almost wholesome.

Sterling thought she'd never looked more beautiful.

As he stepped into the room, she raised her finger to her lips, signaling him to be quiet.

He scowled. As many times as he'd snuck into the twins' bedroom, he'd never woken them up. Stealth was practically part of his DNA.

Feeling Asha's gaze on him, he walked over to the matching fire-truck toddler beds where his grandsons slept peacefully. Normally he stayed and watched them for a while, basking in the adorable little noises they made in their sleep. But with Asha watching him from across the room, he suddenly felt too self-conscious to linger at the boys' bedside. So he settled for kissing their foreheads and adjusting their brightly patterned blankets.

Asha followed him out of the room, shutting the door quietly behind them. "I think Matthew does karate in his sleep," she whispered with a soft smile.

Sterling chuckled. "Michael was the same way. That boy slept so wild we could never keep a blanket on him."

"Hmm. That's the sign of a restless spirit."

"Think so?" Sterling pondered his firstborn son, who changed girlfriends the way he changed underwear. If that didn't qualify as "restless," nothing did.

"He needs a good woman," Asha murmured. "Someone to keep him grounded."

Sterling's eyes narrowed. "I hope to hell you're not volunteering yourself."

Her chin lifted in defiance. "And if I were?"

"Woman, have you lost your damn mind?"

"Keep your voice down!" Asha hissed, glancing up and down the darkened corridor.

Gritting his teeth, Sterling said in a low, controlled voice, "You'd better not have any crazy ideas about sinking your claws into Michael. You're not right for him."

"Says who?"

"Me!"

Without realizing it, they'd walked toward the master suite on the opposite wing of the second floor.

"*If* I were interested in dating Michael," Asha said seethingly, "that would be none of your damn business, Sterling Wolf. You have no say—"

Something snapped inside Sterling. Before he could stop himself, he cupped her face in his hands and kissed her. Hard and possessively.

After several moments—the sweetest, most pleasurable moments he'd enjoyed in ages—Asha broke the kiss and staggered back, staring at him in wide-eyed shock.

Mortified by his actions, Sterling hung his head in sheepish contrition. "Aw, hell. I'm sorry. I don't know what came over—"

Asha lunged at him, throwing her arms around his neck and crushing her soft mouth to his.

With a muffled groan of hunger, Sterling swept her into his arms and carried her to his bedroom.

Chapter 12

The scene at the breakfast table the next morning would have been good material for a sociological study on human dynamics.

In an ironic role reversal from last night, Reese was sullen and subdued while Michael bantered cheerfully with his family. His upbeat mood rankled her, taunting her with memories of their illicit moonlight encounter—an encounter that had left her body thrumming with sexual tension and frustration for the rest of the night.

Every time Michael laughed or flashed one of his killer grins, Reese wanted to stab him with her fork. Once, when he'd caught her glaring at him, he'd smiled and winked at her. If small children hadn't been present, she might have given him the finger.

But Michael wasn't the only one in an exceptionally good mood. Marcus and Samara were back to stealing private smiles at each other, while Sterling was so jovial and relaxed that if Reese didn't know better, she would think Marcus wasn't the *only* member of the Wolf pack who'd gotten laid last night.

In sharp contrast, Celeste was silent and grim faced, shooting dirty looks at Asha throughout the meal. But Asha seemed unconcerned, exuding an aura of serenity that repelled any and all daggers thrown her way.

Only Grant, buried behind a newspaper, seemed oblivious to all the undercurrents at the table. When Celeste discreetly nudged him at one point, he set aside the paper with a sheepish grin and reached for his coffee mug. As he drank, he appeared to be casting about for something to contribute to the conversation.

Finally, he blurted the first thing that obviously came to mind: "That sure was a beautiful full moon last night."

"Sure was," Michael agreed, his wicked gaze meeting Reese's. She hated herself for blushing.

Marcus smiled lazily. "You know what they say. Strange things happen when there's a full moon."

Sterling chuckled into his coffee. "Ain't that the truth."

Asha choked on the orange juice she'd been sipping.

"Are you okay, Mom?" Samara asked in concern.

Asha nodded quickly, her dark eyes glimmering with mirth as she set down her glass and delicately fanned her face with her hand. Celeste frowned.

Marcus grinned at his father and brother. "Hey, remember what we used to do on our camping and fishing trips? Whenever there was a full moon, we'd all sit around the campfire—"

"—and howl at the moon," Sterling and Michael finished, laughing.

"Is that where Michael got his famous howl from?" Reese asked curiously, still not addressing him directly.

Sterling grinned. "If anything, *we* got it from him. Starting from the time he was five years old, he'd always howl after eating something he really liked. So we started putting food into two categories—there was *good,* and then there was *howlin' good.*"

Reese smiled at Michael, so charmed by the anecdote that she temporarily forgot she was supposed to be mad at him. "So that's how you came up with the name of your show."

He nodded, his eyes glinting with amused satisfaction. As if he, too, realized that she'd let her guard down.

"Needless to say," Celeste chimed in, brightening for the first time all morning, "whenever my cooking received one of Michael's coveted 'howlin' good' ratings, I strutted around for the rest of the day like I was Julia Child."

Everyone laughed.

Reese didn't miss the smug glance Celeste shot at Asha, while Grant looked pleased that his innocuous comment had generated such a lively discussion.

Unable to resist an opportunity to make Michael squirm, Reese said ever so innocently, "Someday I'd love to hear the *other* story behind the howl."

"What other story?" Sterling asked.

Everyone looked inquiringly at Michael, whose expression had gone carefully blank.

"Oh, come on, Michael," Reese prompted in a deceptively puzzled voice, as if she couldn't understand why he was playing dumb. "You know the story I'm talking about. Remember? The one Quentin said would offend my feminine sensibilities?"

Celeste gasped. "Michael Sterling Wolf," she scolded, as only a scandalized mother could.

As Michael ducked his head, laughter erupted around the table.

From beneath the thick veil of his lashes, he gave Reese a look that promised retribution. She responded with a huge, triumphant grin.

She'd already learned that when it came to besting this man, she'd take whatever victories she could get. Because she knew they'd be few and far between.

Reese's cell phone rang as she stepped through the front door that evening, her arms laden with shopping bags. Bump-

ing the door closed with her hip, she divested herself of her
baggage and fumbled the phone out of her handbag on the
final ring.

"Hello?" she answered breathlessly.

"Hey." Michael's deep voice poured into her ear.

And just like that, her knees went weak.

Dragging her fingers through her hair, she made her way
into the living room and sank into the nearest chair. "I just
got home," she said in lieu of a greeting.

"I know."

"You know?" She glanced around, half expecting to find
him lurking in the shadows with his phone pressed to his
ear.

Michael chuckled, as if he'd intercepted her paranoid
thoughts. "I just spoke to Marcus. Samara had called to tell
him that they were dropping you off and would be home
soon."

"I see. And had you already instructed Marcus to call and
give you a heads-up?"

"Pretty much." There was a smile in his voice. "How was
the shopping trip?"

She sighed. "Fun. Exhausting. I see why Lenox Square
Mall is considered the Shopping Mecca of the South. And
Asha wore me and Samara out."

Michael chuckled. "And she's the older one. What's wrong
with that picture?"

Reese grinned. "What can I say? The woman was in her
element."

"I can imagine. So, did you get something pretty?"

"I got *a lot* of something pretty," Reese said laughingly,
surveying the mountain of bags bearing the emblems of glitzy,
upscale shops. Not only had Asha handpicked every outfit
for her—the woman knew fashion like nobody's business—
she'd also footed the bill for the entire shopping excursion.
Though Reese had vigorously protested, Asha had refused to
take no for an answer. And, as expected, they'd received red-
carpet treatment everywhere they went, greeted by gushing

salespeople who'd tripped over themselves to do Asha's bidding. The first time they were served champagne, Reese had gaped at Samara, who'd shrugged and grinned, saying, "It's a pain in the ass, but you get used to it."

Reese didn't see how that was remotely possible. Though she'd thoroughly enjoyed shopping with Asha, the dizzying pace of the experience had left her craving a hot, relaxing bath and a glass of chilled wine.

But first she had to get Michael off the phone.

She opened her mouth to tell him good-night, but what came out instead was "Where are you, anyway?"

"At the restaurant."

"You've been there all day?"

"Yeah."

She slipped off her flat sandals and rubbed her sore feet, thinking of their sublimely sensual midnight encounter. It alarmed her to realize that this man, whom she hardly knew, could possess such mastery of her body. If they ever made love, she'd be ruined forever.

"I don't hear a lot of noise in the background," she observed.

"That's because I'm sitting on the balcony," Michael murmured. "At our table."

Our table. The words reverberated in her mind as a melting warmth spread through her, a deep longing.

She forced out a laugh that sounded strangled to her own ears. "So now we have a table?"

"Yeah," he said huskily. "We do."

"Come on," she scoffed. "Do you really expect me to believe you've never taken another woman up to the balcony?"

"You're the first, Reese."

God help her, she believed him. Closing her eyes, she drew a deep, shaky breath and slowly exhaled. "Michael…"

"I need you—"

"Michael."

"—to come down to the restaurant."

Her eyes snapped open. That was the last thing she'd expected him to say. "You need me to do what?"

"Come to the restaurant. That's actually the reason I was calling. If you want to be my apprentice, you should familiarize yourself with the inner workings of a restaurant. So tonight I'm giving you a front-row seat to our busy kitchen."

Reese groaned. "That sounds lovely, Michael, but does it have to be *tonight?*"

"Tonight's perfect. Tuesdays are generally our slowest nights, so it won't be a complete madhouse. Besides, aren't you the one who said you were trying to get into your new role as my apprentice?"

The man remembered everything, damn him. "I did, and I am. But tonight doesn't work for me."

"Tonight, Reese."

"Oh, come on, Michael," she wheedled. "It's already after seven. And Asha ran me ragged today. My feet are *killing* me."

He laughed. "Don't ever whine to a chef about having sore feet after a leisurely afternoon of shopping. Trust me, you won't get any sympathy."

She bit her lip, feeling a pang of shame. "I guess you *have* been on your feet all day, slaving in a hot kitchen."

"That's right, and you don't hear me complaining. So suck it up, buttercup."

Reese heaved a dramatic sigh of resignation. "All right. I'm coming, I'm coming."

"Mmm," came his low, husky rumble. "Now that's what I like to hear."

Heat stung her cheeks at the sexual innuendo. "Down, boy."

"Too late." He chuckled. "Anyway, your cab should be there in a few minutes."

"*What?* You already called me a cab?"

"Yeah. I'll drive you home afterward."

Her hackles rose. "Don't you think it was a bit presumptuous of you to call a cab before you'd even spoken to me?"

"Absolutely." He was infuriatingly unapologetic. "Look, babe, I have to go. I'll see you when you get here."

Reese sputtered in protest, but he'd already hung up on her.

When she arrived at the restaurant thirty minutes later, Michael met her outside, looking good enough to eat in his crisp white chef's jacket. He helped her out of the cab, then paid and tipped the driver so generously that the man's eyes lit up like he'd just won a million-dollar jackpot.

As the taxi lurched off down the street, Michael and Reese lingered on the sidewalk, gazing at each other. He touched her face, smiling warmly into her eyes. "Hi."

Her insides melted. "Hi."

"Glad you came."

She made a wry face. "You didn't give me much of a choice, slave driver."

Chuckling, he took her by the hand and led her inside.

Reese glanced around the crowded restaurant in disbelief. "I thought you said Tuesdays are slow."

Michael slanted her a grin. "This *is* slow."

He hung a right, ushering her down a short corridor to the kitchen. Just beyond the swinging door was a fast-paced world of sweat, stress and chaos punctuated by the noisy clang of pots and pans.

Michael escorted Reese through the bustling labyrinth of work spaces to a semiprivate area partitioned off by a long, stainless steel table. From there she'd have an up-close-and-personal view of the action without getting in the way.

Moments after she'd sat down, Michael set a steaming plate before her. Reese's mouth watered as the most heavenly aroma wafted up her nostrils.

"What's this?" she breathed, eyeing the appetizing meal.

"Another house specialty. Bourbon-glazed pork tenderloin with caramelized plantains."

"Oh my."

"When was the last time you ate?"

"Eons ago. We stopped for an early lunch."

"Good. Then I expect you to clean your plate."

"Don't have to tell *me* twice," Reese said, already seizing her fork.

Michael smiled as he poured her a glass of wine.

"Riesling," she said wonderingly. "You remembered."

"Of course." His smile deepened. "I remember everything."

She grinned. "Don't *I* know it."

He winked at her. "I'll be back to check up on you later. Enjoy the show."

And what a show it was, a riveting choreography of cuisine that was unlike anything Reese had ever seen before. As a self-professed foodie, she'd always assumed she knew what went on behind the scenes of a busy restaurant. Now, with a front-row seat to one of the most famous kitchens in the country, she realized how little she'd understood about the level of coordination that went into preparing an entrée before it was served to customers. And everyone, from the line cooks to the sous chef, knew their roles and executed them with brisk efficiency.

It came as no surprise to Reese that Michael's kitchen ran like a well-oiled machine. Though he was clearly in charge, he didn't yell at his crew like some obnoxious, foulmouthed tyrant. He barked orders, but he was never obscene. He scowled when mistakes were made, but he never spared praise. He was intensely focused, but he could disarm with a sudden grin and a joke that drew raucous laughter. He didn't have to resort to bullying for his commanding presence to be felt throughout the kitchen. His employees understood that he demanded perfection, and they did their damnedest to deliver it.

What *did* surprise Reese was how hands-on Michael was. He made a final inspection of every plate that went out and usually added finishing touches—a garnish of celery leaves on lobster, an artful drizzle of sauce over a chicken dish. Unlike many other celebrity chefs who owned restaurants,

Michael was no figurehead. He *was* the heart and soul of Wolf's Soul.

The hours flew by. Before Reese knew it, it was eleven o'clock and the restaurant was closed. While Michael was out front seeing off the last of his customers, she shocked the staff by pitching in to clean up the kitchen, overriding their protests. Michael returned to the sight of her elbow deep in a sink full of dishes, laughing in response to someone's off-color joke.

When his employees glanced around and saw him frozen in the doorway with an arrested expression on his face, they sobered at once, no doubt afraid they'd get in trouble for allowing his guest to wash dishes. Undaunted, Reese met Michael's gaze with a look of haughty defiance, silently daring him to reprimand anyone.

Without a word he went to work emptying a trash bin, and the clean-up efforts continued in cheerful camaraderie until the kitchen was spotless.

After everyone had gone home, Reese and Michael collapsed into chairs at the prep table, exhaling sighs of happy exhaustion.

"What a day," Reese declared, kicking off her sandals.

Michael grinned, propping his big, booted feet on the table and lounging back. "Nothing like an honest day's work. Well—at least for one of us."

"Hey!" Reese laughingly protested, slapping him playfully on the leg. "Shopping with Asha Dubois *is* work!"

"Right," he drawled, mouth twitching. "I'm sure it was *really* strenuous for you, lifting those glasses of champagne to your lips and lugging around all those *heavy* boxes of designer shoes. Poor baby. You're gonna need weeks to recover."

Reese tried to glare at him, but the amusement won out. Throwing back her head, she laughed so hard that tears leaked from the corners of her eyes. Watching her, Michael couldn't help laughing.

Long moments later, they were still grinning and shaking their heads at each other.

"All kidding aside," Michael said, sobering. "Thanks for helping out tonight. That was totally…unexpected."

Reese shrugged dismissively. "I figured it was the least I could do, after I sat around all night stuffing my face while everyone else busted their asses."

He smiled a little. "Seriously though, Reese. It was a very thoughtful gesture, and I could tell it really meant a lot to my staff. So…thank you."

"You're welcome." The earnestness in his voice made her heart do a weird fluttering thing. Gazing at him, she blurted impetuously, "I think you're amazing."

Something soft flickered in his dark eyes.

Her face flushed, and she hastened to elaborate. "I mean, uh, the way you interact with your crew is amazing. You guys have such amazing chemistry. Cohesion. It was like watching a beautifully choreographed ballet—except with noise and shooting flames from a grill."

Michael chuckled. "I don't think anyone's ever put it quite that way before."

"No?" She grinned. "Maybe I *should* be a restaurant critic."

They looked at each other, then laughed. Reese marveled that they could find humor in something that had nearly led to bloodshed just a week ago.

"Hey," she said, struck by a sudden realization. "I ate here for the first time last Tuesday!"

"I know." Michael smiled lazily at her. "I thought you'd remember that when I told you Tuesdays were slow."

She grinned ruefully. "I wasn't thinking about that. I was too busy trying to weasel my way out of leaving the house."

"Aren't you glad I didn't let you?"

"I am. I thoroughly enjoyed myself tonight. Being able to watch you guys at work was a real treat. And speaking of treats, everything was absolutely delicious, Michael. The bourbon-glazed pork tenderloin was to die for. And that Kahlua mousse made by your pastry chef was divine. I have to get the recipe."

Michael chuckled drily. "Considering that Gerard has a crush on you, he'd probably give you any recipe you wanted. In all the years he's worked here, I've never seen him make a special dessert for anyone."

Reese sighed. "After one taste of that mousse, I think I fell a little in love myself."

"Well, hell, if *that's* all it takes, wait till you try my triple chocolate cheesecake."

"Mmmm." She gave him a demure smile. "Are you trying to make me fall in love with you, Michael?"

His gaze darkened. "Maybe I am."

Reese stared at him, her heart thudding.

Slowly, one by one, he removed his feet from the table and sat up in the chair.

She didn't know who moved first.

It must have been her, for the next thing she knew, she was straddling his lap as they kissed deeply and feverishly. She locked her fingers behind his nape and sucked his lush bottom lip into her mouth, making him groan hoarsely. He shoved her flirty summer skirt up her thighs and ran his hands up to her hips, where he held her tightly against his raging erection. She moaned and writhed desperately against him.

Breaking the kiss, he yanked off her halter top and deftly unfastened the front hook of her bra. Her full breasts spilled into his hands, her nipples already distended with arousal. He made a feral sound deep in his throat and cupped her, massaging and caressing. She cried out with shocked pleasure as his mouth came down to suck in a nipple. Heat pooled between her legs.

Abruptly he surged to his feet and lifted her onto the high table. She spread her thighs eagerly and he stepped between them. She shrugged off her bra, let it fall away.

Gazes locked, they both attacked the knotted buttons on his chef's jacket. There were double rows of them. Way too damn many. Reese cursed in frustration, her fingers fumbling in her urgency to get at his skin. Even with his own hands flying over the buttons with practiced efficiency, it wasn't fast enough for her.

"Hurry," she pleaded in a breathless, lusty voice she hardly recognized as her own. *"Hurry."*

Michael laughed, dark and wicked.

She crooned with exhilaration as he tore the jacket off his broad shoulders and tossed it aside. Seeing that he wore a white T-shirt underneath, she scowled at yet another barrier. Together she and Michael tugged the shirt up and over his head. And then he was on display for her, his wide, powerful chest ridged with muscle beneath glorious mahogany skin. In helpless fascination, she ran her hands over him, her fingers grazing the intricate tattoo that curled around his muscled bicep. He watched her through heavy-lidded eyes, a faint tremor passing through him as she slowly traced the ink outline of Greek letters.

He lowered his head and took her mouth in a deep, hungry kiss, whispering, "I love the way you touch me."

"And I love to touch you," she whispered back.

He groaned, his eyes glittering with fierce arousal as he pushed her skirt out of the way. She raised her hips a little as he pulled her panties down over her hips and off her legs. She watched as he brought the scrap of black lace to his nose and inhaled, his eyes rolling closed as he savored her scent. It was *such* an erotic gesture that she nearly came out of her skin, her blood heated so fast.

He set her panties down on the table, as if he wanted to keep them within easy reach. Holding her gaze, he trailed his middle finger up her inner thigh, leaving a path of scorched nerve endings. She gasped as he stroked her clitoris, which was as hard and erect as her nipples. He didn't taunt her this time about the hot river of need that flowed between her thighs. Tonight wasn't about scoring points.

Tonight was about heeding raw animal instinct.

Reese didn't want a gentle seduction. She wanted hard, fast pounding, a driving rhythm that would quench the fire raging in her blood. And she knew that this man could—and *would*—deliver.

She went for his belt at the same time he did, their fingers tangling in their haste to get him unbuckled and unzipped. She shoved down his dark trousers and briefs, gasping as his penis sprang free. It was impressively long, thick and hard. The swollen head glistened with pre-come, and a solitary vein bulged beneath the granite-smooth dark skin. It was the most beautiful thing Reese had ever seen. Her loins contracted in hungry response.

But before she could reach down to stroke him, he dug inside his pants pocket and fished out his wallet. She almost sobbed with relief when she saw the flash of a foil packet. He ripped it open with his teeth and quickly smoothed the condom over his erection. She moaned and shamelessly rubbed her hips against him, desperate to have him inside her. She'd waited long enough, past the point of endurance.

As he dragged her to the very edge of the table, she wrapped her arms around his neck and clamped her thighs around his hips. They stared into each other's eyes as he slid slowly into her. She cried out at the exquisite fullness of him, stretching her as he seated himself to the hilt.

A shudder ripped through his big body and he groaned. Bracing his arms on either side of her on the table, he closed his eyes in an expression of unadulterated ecstasy.

Reese tightened her thighs around him, savoring the profound intimacy of the moment. A moment unlike anything she'd ever experienced before.

Slowly his eyes opened and he began moving inside her, a deep, languorous glide that heightened her anticipation and promised unspeakable pleasures. She moaned and gripped his shoulders, her fingertips digging into the hard pad of muscle.

As his strokes deepened, he stared into her eyes with a burning ferocity that intensified the ache in her womb.

"I knew it'd be this way between us," he whispered thickly.

"We both knew it the moment we saw each other for the first time."

Reese could only manage a whimper, beyond any and all rational thought.

Soon the tempo of his thrusts increased, sending her breasts bouncing up and down. He bent, sucking them into his mouth in hot, greedy pulls. She mewled and ground her pelvis against his, her nails raking his broad back. He raised his head and seized her lips. They kissed in raw urgency, their mouths fusing, tongues twining. She was frantic with need, a slave to his masterful possession of her body. He owned her, and he knew it.

He grasped her bottom and lifted her off the table, forcing her to absorb the full impact of his heavy body pounding into hers. Over his shoulder, she caught sight of his taut, round butt in a mirror on the opposite wall. The image of his muscles clenching and unclenching as he thrust into her was something straight out of her most erotic fantasies. She grew aroused beyond all bearing.

She grabbed his butt, her hips pumping wildly as she met the driving force of each stroke. He groaned, throwing back his head and closing his eyes. A fine sheen of perspiration coated his dark skin. Her gaze was riveted to a trickle of sweat that rolled down his quivering stomach muscles and disappeared between their joined bodies.

They rocked and glided against each other, their guttural cries and moans echoing around the large kitchen. Reese's heart thundered, her skin burned everywhere. A full, delicious pressure was gathering velocity in her loins.

Michael set her back down on the table and drew her legs higher around his torso, as high as they could go without wrapping around his neck. His eyes blazed black as coal as he drove into her ruthlessly, plunging so deep she felt the vibrations in the back of her womb. She keened with pleasure. Her body soared higher, the pressure building to fever pitch.

With one last powerful thrust, he sent her hurtling into an orgasm of cataclysmic proportions. She threw back her head and screamed his name as her inner muscles pulsed and contracted with the explosive spasms.

A moment later Michael came with a primal shout, his hips bucking furiously as he rode her through his violent release.

They clutched each other tightly, his face buried in the damp curve of her neck, their bodies shaking, their breath sawing in and out of their lungs.

Reese didn't know how much time passed. She didn't care. Wrapped in Michael's strong arms, with his throbbing penis sheathed inside her and his heart drumming against hers, she could have clung to him forever.

At length they drew apart and stared at each other with identical expressions of awe.

Reese trembled as he stroked a hand over her hair and brushed a tender kiss across her cheek, then her mouth.

"Beautiful Reese," he murmured in a voice that reached deep into her soul. "There's no turning back now."

Her heart swelled to aching. She closed her eyes against a hot sting of tears.

Then, and only then, did she remember Victor.

God help me, she thought. *What have I done?*

Chapter 13

When Michael awoke the next morning, the first thing he became aware of was the lush, silky warmth of Reese's body curved snugly against his, as if they were interlocked pieces of a puzzle. A perfect fit.

As he came more fully awake, he made another stunning discovery.

He was in the same spot he'd been in when he'd drifted off to sleep after making love to Reese last night. The *exact* same spot. He knew because the covers weren't twisted around his legs or hanging off the bed, as he usually found them in the mornings. No, they were still resting at his waist, undisturbed. Which could only mean one thing.

He hadn't moved all night.

But that's impossible, his mind rebelled.

For as long as Michael could remember, he'd always been a fitful sleeper. His mother used to tell him that as a newborn, the only way she could get him to sleep for a few hours was to keep him latched onto her breast. The moment she stopped feeding him, he'd wriggle himself right awake. As he grew older, his parents had often entered his room to find him huddled in the middle of the bed and shivering in his sleep because he'd kicked off the covers.

Over the years he'd lost count of how many women had accused him of retreating to his side of the bed and not snuggling with them during the night. He'd grown so tired of hearing the same complaint that he'd stopped spending the night with his lovers, getting up and leaving them shortly after sex. Sure, it made him seem callous and selfish, but he figured that was the best way to spare their feelings in the long run.

He wasn't a sound sleeper. Never would be. So spooning a woman during the night was out of the question.

Yet there he was spooning Reese. And, apparently, he'd done it all night.

I'll be damned, Michael thought, shaken by the discovery.

It was just one more example of the way Reese was turning his world upside down. Before meeting her, he'd had no concept of what it meant to be obsessed with a woman, to crave her so badly that nearly every waking thought was consumed with her. But over the past week he'd received a crash course in obsession, and he was proving to be quite an apt pupil.

As vivid memories from last night flooded his mind, he couldn't keep a slow, wicked smile off his face. After their explosive interlude at the restaurant—would he ever see his precious kitchen the same way again?—he'd somehow convinced Reese to spend the night with him. Though she'd seemed a bit subdued on the ride to his penthouse, once he took her in his arms again, she'd surrendered with the same desperate abandon as before. They hadn't even made it upstairs to his bedroom before he'd had her long legs wrapped around him as he thrust into her. He'd made love to her over and over again throughout the night. He was insatiable, couldn't get enough of her.

As if to demonstrate, his penis hardened in response to the lush swell of her bottom nestled against his lap. He grinned, already contemplating several creative ways he could wake her up—all involving the use of his hands, lips and tongue.

But as he edged closer to her, Reese suddenly tensed and shifted away from him.

His grin faded. Was she already awake?

Propping himself up on one elbow, he peered down into her face. Sure enough, her eyes were open as she stared straight ahead.

He leaned down and pressed an openmouthed kiss to her silky bare shoulder. A fine tremor passed through her, and her long lashes fluttered. He felt a glimmer of hope.

"Good morning," he murmured.

She didn't turn to look at him. "Good morning."

"Did you sleep well?"

She hesitated, then nodded reluctantly.

"I did, too. Slept like a baby, in fact." It was true. He couldn't remember the last time he'd ever enjoyed such a deep, sated slumber. And he'd awakened feeling refreshed and blissfully content. He could definitely get used to more mornings like this.

Provided he got the opportunity.

Smiling down at Reese, he gently combed his fingers through the thick, lustrous strands of black hair fanned out across her pillow. She closed her eyes, but not in languid pleasure. She looked strained, as if she were waging an internal battle.

He found himself holding his breath, wondering which side would win.

A long, taut silence stretched between them.

When Michael couldn't take it anymore, he decided his only option was to tackle the unwelcome elephant in the room.

"You're having second thoughts about last night."

Reese's eyes opened. She hesitated, then nodded tightly. "It was a mistake."

Anger flared inside his chest. "It sure as hell didn't *feel* like a mistake."

It was the wrong thing to say, the wrong approach to use.

She scooted away from him and sat up quickly, clutching the sheet protectively to her chest. Her cheeks were still flushed from hours of savage lovemaking, her lips were still swollen from hard kissing, her hair was tousled about her face and shoulders, and beneath the sheet, her voluptuous breasts beckoned to him. She was incredibly beautiful.

And too damned tempting for her own good.

Michael reached for her. "Reese—"

She jerked away from him.

Swearing under his breath, Michael fell back against his stack of pillows and blew out a harsh, frustrated breath. This wasn't going the way he'd hoped. He'd been looking forward to spending a few more pleasurable hours in bed with her. And then he'd imagined them cooking breakfast together, dividing the tasks, making a game of "accidentally" bumping into each other as they worked. He'd envisioned them laughing, teasing, stealing kisses as they carried their plates out to the balcony to enjoy the scenic view.

But maybe his expectations had been as unrealistic as those of the women who'd wanted him to cuddle with them during the night.

Exhaling a shaky breath, Reese dragged a hand through her hair. "You should take me home now."

"*No.* Not yet." Michael was surprised—and slightly appalled—by the note of desperation he heard in his voice. What the hell was wrong with him? Since when did *he* beg a woman to stay after sex?

Reese looked at him, those dark cat eyes roving across his face in silent appraisal. She seemed to be taking his measure, weighing an important decision in her mind.

He stared back at her, waiting.

After a prolonged moment she glanced away and shook her head at the ceiling. "I owe you an apology."

Of all the things he'd expected her to say, *that* wasn't one of them. He stared at her in surprise. "What do you have to apologize for?" he asked carefully.

She tugged her plump lower lip through her teeth. "I haven't been myself lately," she confessed.

"Who have you been?"

"A woman who doesn't know what she wants. A confused, indecisive woman." She grimaced. "The kind of woman I've always disliked and strived not to be."

Intrigued by the self-deprecating words, Michael shifted onto his side to face her, propping his head in his hand. "Why don't you know what you want?" he asked quietly.

She sighed heavily. "It's complicated."

"It doesn't have to be."

"Believe me, I wish that were true." She heaved another resigned breath. "Anyway, the reason I owe you an apology is that I've been giving you mixed signals since the night we met. I say one thing and do the complete opposite. Spending the night with you was the behemoth of all mixed signals."

"You don't hear me complaining," Michael drawled.

"Of course not," she muttered, throwing him a sardonic look. "You've been a willing accomplice."

He arched a brow. "Accomplice? Have we committed a crime here?"

"I almost wish we had," she groaned, covering her face with her hands.

Michael pretended to take umbrage. "I think you're the first woman who's ever told me that committing a crime would be preferable to making love with me. There goes my ego."

A muffled laugh escaped her. "Oh, hush. You know what I meant."

He smiled lazily.

Uncovering her face, she shot him a shy glance under her lashes. "Don't get me wrong, Michael. Last night was amazing—"

"That doesn't even begin to describe it."

She blushed deeply, averting her gaze. "You're right. *Amazing* doesn't do justice to what we shared last night. It was…unforgettable. But that doesn't change the fact that it was a mistake."

His breath hissed through his teeth. "Here we go again. The damn boyfriend."

"Yes!" she burst out, her dark eyes snapping angrily. "I have a boyfriend, a fact that you seem unwilling or incapable of respecting."

Michael flinched. Her words had struck a raw nerve, forcing him to acknowledge how easily he'd abandoned his long-held convictions. Maybe he and Grant Rutherford were more alike than he'd thought. Like his stepfather, Michael had pursued and seduced Reese, flagrantly disregarding the other man in her life. Although the obvious difference here was that Reese wasn't married with children, his behavior was still deplorable by his own standards.

Agitated, he scrubbed his hands over his face and muttered a vicious oath under his breath.

Reese moved to slide out of the bed. "I really should—"

Michael's arm shot out, forestalling her retreat with a hand on her thigh. Beneath the covers, she quivered at his touch.

"Wait," he growled, sitting up quickly. "You don't have to leave. Let's talk about this, damn it. How serious is this thing between you and that dude?"

Jerking her leg out of his grasp, she snapped, "I'm not going to discuss my boyfriend with you."

That was probably for the best, Michael mused grimly. The thought of her being with another man—giving herself to him with the same passion and abandon with which she'd surrendered to Michael—filled him with a possessive fury that was unlike anything he'd ever felt before.

Yeah, he definitely didn't need to know the specific details of her relationship with what's-his-face. Still, he couldn't resist demanding, "Are you guys on the outs or what? I mean, he sent you two dozen roses and asked you to come back to him."

"So you *did* read the card!" Reese pounced accusingly. "I knew it. You had no right!"

Michael scowled. "It fell on the floor. It's not as if I went digging through the box to find it."

"You could have handed it to me without reading it!"

"I could have, but I didn't. Anyway, that's not the point. I asked you a question. Are you and Victor having a lovers' quarrel? Are you breaking up with him?"

"No!" she hissed furiously.

Disappointment knifed through Michael. He held her flashing gaze a moment longer, then eased back against his pillows and folded his arms behind his head, a deceptively relaxed pose.

Silence lapsed between them. This time he wouldn't be the one to break it.

And he wasn't.

"I'm not a cheater."

Michael turned his head on the pillow to look at Reese. She'd spoken so softly he wasn't sure he'd heard her right. "What did you say?"

"I'm not a cheater." A wry, humorless smile turned up one side of her mouth. "I know that sounds hard to believe under the present circumstances, but I generally pride myself on being faithful."

She sounded so forlorn that Michael felt a twinge of sympathy—and guilt. "We can't always control who we're attracted to, sweetheart," he murmured.

Her lips twisted cynically. "That's such a typical male thing to say. How many poor women have you fed that line?"

He bristled. "It's not a line. It's the damn truth."

"Riiight." Still clutching the sheet to her body, she drew her knees up to her chest, as if she needed another barrier between them. Suddenly she looked very small and vulnerable in the enormous bed.

A surge of protective tenderness rushed through Michael. "Did someone cheat on you, Reese?"

She sighed heavily. "I don't need to have experienced it to know that cheating is wrong."

Michael frowned. "You aren't cheating."

"No? Then what do you call it?"

"Exploring your options."

That wrung a grim laugh out of her. "Let's not kid ourselves,

Michael. As unforgettable as last night was, we both know it was nothing more than a one-night stand."

"You're wrong," he said mildly. "By its very definition, the term 'one-night stand' could never apply to us."

"And why is that?" she challenged.

He leaned forward, his voice dropping to a silky murmur. "Because I intend to have you again. And again. *And again.*"

Her breath hitched, and he watched in satisfaction as her dark gaze went to his mouth, then roamed over his bare chest before lowering to where his erection tented the covers at his waist. Heat flared in her eyes. Above the top edge of the sheet, her breasts heaved as she struggled to regulate her erratic breathing.

"No, Michael," she whispered.

"*Yes,* Reese."

Their gazes held for another long, sexually charged moment before she glanced away, expelling a shaky breath. "This is ridiculous," she mumbled. "You're not listening to me. I just explained to you why this was a mistake, and why it can't happen again."

"And *I'm* telling you that it can, and it will."

"What's the point?" she burst out in exasperation. "You and I both know this isn't leading anywhere! In less than two months I'll be back in Houston, and you'll be back to enjoying your status as one of the country's most eligible bachelors. Why ruin lives over what essentially amounts to a summer fling?"

"This ain't no damn summer fling," Michael snarled, incensed by her repeated attempts to trivialize what may have been the most spectacular night of his life.

"Oh, come on, Michael," she scoffed. "Why are you making such a big deal out of this? I mean, you're *Michael Wolf.* You can have any woman you want, whenever you want, wherever you—"

Something snapped inside him, and he exploded, "I don't want *any* woman! I want you!"

Reese stared at him, her eyes wide with stunned disbelief.

He glared back at her, his jaw tightly clenched as he fought for self-control. His heart was hammering against his ribs, and his entire body was vibrating with the fierce, overpowering urge to pin her to the mattress and make love to her in a way that would leave no doubt in her mind that she belonged to him.

"Oh my." Reese bit her lip, shaking her head slowly at him. "You really *are* going to make me fall in love with you, aren't you?"

Michael's pulse thudded. An emotion suspiciously akin to hope sprang to life in his chest. And then he saw a trace of amusement glittering in her eyes.

"What's so damned funny?" he snapped.

"You. Me. *Us.*" She sighed, shaking her head again. "The truth is, Michael, I've been halfway in love with you for the past three years. My family, friends and colleagues tease me constantly about having a major crush on you. It's so bad that they've even taken to calling you my fantasy boyfriend."

Michael wasn't amused. "So what are you saying? Last night was about you living out some sort of fantasy?"

Reese gave a low, indulgent laugh. "Oh, now, don't give me that wounded look. You have no reason to be offended. What we shared last night far exceeded my fantasies, and I didn't think that was even possible. But just because you rocked my world doesn't mean I foolishly expect you to become my boyfriend."

"And why the hell not?" Michael growled. "What would be so damn crazy about that?"

She gave him a gentle, almost pitying look. "Come on, Michael. You're not *real*-boyfriend material. You're *fantasy*-boyfriend material. You're that smokin' hot guy every girl fantasizes about. The guy who, though you know he's totally unattainable, you'd jump at the chance to spend one wild night of sex with. And then years down the line—long after you'd settled into a comfortable life with the safe, sweet, reliable man you ended up marrying—you'd indulge in a moment of girlish whim and tell your daughters all about that one reckless night of passion you had with your fantasy lover." She smiled demurely. "I'm lucky. Not every woman gets such an opportunity."

Michael glowered at her, seething with anger and something darker, something infinitely more dangerous. Something that made his heart ache with fierce, primal yearning.

Reese's smile wavered. "Uh, Michael—?"

He lunged at her just as a cell phone suddenly rang, intruding like the blast of an explosion in the room.

Reese scrambled to the other side of the bed, looking as relieved as a small doe that had narrowly escaped the clutches of a savage predator.

Scowling, Michael watched as she reached down, grabbed her phone out of her purse—when the hell had she brought *that* upstairs?—and answered in a breathless rush, "Hello?" Pause. "Yes, this is Reese St. James."

The sheet had become dislodged in her mad scramble to reach the phone. Michael stared, his penis twitching at the sight of her full, luscious breasts crowned with dark nipples. He remembered the delicious weight of them in his hands, remembered the way they'd swelled beneath the hungry lash of his tongue, remembered the way they'd bounced and jiggled as he drove into her.

He reached down to stroke his erection before he caught himself.

Reese listened into the phone for a moment. "Sure. I'll hold." Her eyes lifted to Michael's. "It's—" She broke off at the arrested look on his face. Following the direction of his gaze, she gasped and snatched the sheet back over her breasts.

Michael felt a sharp pang of regret—and annoyance. Who the hell was calling her this early in the morning? It'd *better* not be her damn boyfriend!

"Who's that?" he demanded.

Her eyes narrowed at his jealous, possessive tone. She pressed the mute button on her phone and said coolly, "It's

Drew's assistant. They want me to come down to the studio today for an orientation session, and she also wanted to remind me that you and I are supposed to be shooting our promo spot tomorrow for the apprentice series."

"I don't need a damn reminder." Leaning back against the headboard, Michael gestured impatiently at the phone. "Why are you on hold?"

"She's double-checking some details with the production crew." Reese clutched the sheet tighter to her chest, pinning him with a hostile glare. "I'd like to get dressed."

"Knock yourself out," he muttered, waving in the general vicinity of the adjoining master bathroom.

"My clothes are downstairs," she reminded him.

"So go get them," he retorted, defiantly rebelling against every gentlemanly instinct that had been instilled in him from the time he could walk.

He could almost hear Reese gnashing her teeth. "I'm on the phone," she said tersely. "And if it's all the same to you, I'd rather not wander around your penthouse butt naked. Especially with all these damn windows."

"We're on the fortieth floor. No one can see you."

Her eyes narrowed to dangerous slits. "I'm asking nicely."

"You don't sound very nice to me."

"Pretty please!" she snapped.

Heaving an impatient breath, Michael flung back the covers and swung out of the bed. To demonstrate to Reese that they were safe from the prying eyes of voyeurs, he stalked across the master suite and stood before the wall of windows, just as bold and nude as he pleased.

"See," he said, turning back toward the bed. "It's all g—"

The rest of the words died on his lips.

Eyes filled with raw, naked hunger stared back at him.

His body reacted with a sharp jolt of lust that sizzled through his veins and rushed straight to his groin. His erection, which had taunted him all morning, now hardened into full-fledged arousal.

Reese was utterly riveted.

Driven by some perverse impulse, Michael reached down and trailed his fingers lightly along the jutting length of his shaft. Inwardly he smiled at the soft gasp that came from across the room. Without looking at Reese, he wrapped his fingers around his erection and gave himself a long, stroking caress. Up and down, slowly and provocatively. He let his eyes drift closed, as if he were so caught up in pleasuring himself that he'd completely forgotten he had an audience. A captive audience, judging by the sound of Reese's ragged breathing.

Not that he was entirely immune to the eroticism of being watched by her. As he pumped himself, he imagined that it was her hands sliding along his shaft, as she'd done last night. Stroking, caressing, driving him insane with lust. He became so aroused by the explicit images that a pearly bead of pre-come seeped from the tip of his penis, adding to the realism of his little "performance."

When he finally stole a peek at Reese, her eyes were heavy lidded and glazed with desire, her lips parted on a soundless moan. He felt a surge of wicked triumph that was tempered only by his own mounting arousal.

Giving her a lazy smile, he left the windows and began sauntering from the room.

"Yes, I'm still here," he heard her croak into the phone.

Glancing over his shoulder, he saw her reach beneath the covers to touch herself. As she closed her eyes and released a shuddering breath, he grinned with satisfaction.

Maybe being a fantasy boyfriend wasn't such a bad thing after all.

Chapter 14

"Honey, I'm home!" Raina Mayne announced in a singsong voice that brought a grin to Reese's face on the other end of the phone.

"Hey, you," she greeted her sister, sinking into her favorite armchair in the living room. "How was Italy?"

"Absolutely wonderful," Raina said dreamily.

Reese's grin widened. "I want to hear all about it."

"Well, the conference was productive, of course. I came away with a wealth of information about the latest advances in spa therapy, which I can't wait to incorporate at Touch of Heaven."

"That's good." Reese knew how much her sister's luxury day spa meant to her.

"As great as the conference was," Raina continued, "the other things we did are what made the trip so special. We went on moonlit gondola rides, explored beautiful vineyards. Oh, and the *food,* Reesey. The pasta, those gelatos. You would have been in foodie heaven."

Reese smiled, fighting a small pang of envy. "It all sounds *very* romantic."

"It was. It felt like a second honeymoon." Raina sighed. "You should have been there."

"Oh, I don't think so. I would've been a third wheel. Maybe next time."

"Not as long as you and Victor are together," Raina muttered under her breath.

Reese's smile faded. "What did you say?"

"Nothing," Raina said brightly—too brightly. "Anyway, enough about my trip. How's Hotlanta? Are you having fun?"

"You could say that." Now that Reese finally had her sister on the phone, she didn't even know where to begin. She had so much to tell her. And yet, a part of her wanted to keep the most intimate details of her liaison with Michael to herself, like a cherished secret.

She decided to start somewhere safe. "First and foremost, I have some exciting news to share. Remember the contest I entered six months ago to become Michael Wolf's apprentice?"

Raina snorted out a laugh. "Of course I remember. You were—" She broke off abruptly. "Wait a minute. Are you about to tell me that—"

"You're speaking to Michael Wolf's new apprentice."

"Oh my God!" Raina let out an ear-splitting squeal that must have brought her husband running. Raina excitedly repeated the news to him.

"Hey, that's great," Warrick Mayne's deep, masculine timbre could be heard in the background. "Tell her I said congratulations."

"Warrick says congratulations," Raina quickly relayed.

Reese smiled. "Tell him I said thanks."

"He just left the room. This is unbelievable, Reesey," Raina continued in a breathless rush. "I *knew* that recipe you submitted would knock the judges' socks off. Remember how much we all loved it when you made it for us?"

"Yes. Thanks for being my guinea pigs."

"Hell, *we* should thank *you.* Do Mom and Dad know?"

"Of course. They were very excited. I made them promise to let me tell you."

"Man, why did *I* have to be the last one to find out?" Being the baby of the family, Raina had a complex about being last in *anything.* "When'd you get the call?"

"Tuesday, technically. But I didn't listen to the actual message until Wednesday."

"Today?"

"No, last Wednesday."

"*Last* Wednesday!" Raina cried in disbelief. "You should have called me!"

Reese laughed. "I didn't want to disturb you. Besides, there was a six-hour time difference."

"I don't care! You could have called me any time."

Reese grinned. "Even if you and Warrick were in the middle of, ah…" She trailed off pointedly, clearing her throat.

"Well…" There was no mistaking the naughty mischief in Raina's voice.

Again Reese laughed. "I didn't think so."

"You could have left me a message," Raina insisted. "That's what voice mail is for. Anyway, you must have been thrilled when you got the call."

"Actually," Reese said drily, "I was anything but."

"Why?"

"Well, I'd met Michael Wolf at his restaurant the night before. Let's just say we got off to a rocky start."

Knowing Raina would never accept such a cryptic response, Reese gave her a detailed account of everything that had transpired between her and Michael that night, as well as the next morning when he'd called to apologize to her, only to further antagonize her.

"I can't believe he behaved that way," Raina exclaimed at the end of the story. "Warrick always speaks so highly of Michael Wolf. I wouldn't have expected him to come off as such a jerk. It just goes to show—"

"Wait a minute," Reese interrupted. "What do you mean, Warrick speaks highly of Michael? Warrick knows him?"

"Yes." Raina sounded sheepish. "I've been meaning to tell you for months, but between planning the wedding and opening the new spa, I kept getting sidetracked. And I was also hoping to surprise you when Michael showed up at the wedding. I was *so* disappointed when he couldn't make it. He had to fly to Barcelona to help judge the finale for *Top Chef* or one of those other cooking shows. But he sent us the most amazing wedding gift—"

"How do he and Warrick know each other?" Reese interrupted again.

"They met through a professional organization for engineers. You know, of course, that Michael was a successful engineer in his previous life. At any rate, he and Warrick really hit it off and have been friends ever since."

"Wow," Reese whispered. "Talk about six degrees of separation."

"I know. So, uh, you're not mad at me for not telling you sooner?" Raina said meekly.

"No." Reese smiled. "It's obvious Michael and I were destined to meet eventually, anyway."

"Obviously." Raina chuckled. "Don't think I wasn't going to comment on the fact that you almost slept with him the first night you met him. That is *so* unlike you, Reesey. That man must be even finer in person."

"Words can't begin to describe," Reese murmured.

She shuddered at the memory of Michael gilded in sunlight as he stood before his bedroom windows—gloriously naked and fully aroused. When he'd begun stroking himself, it was all Reese could do not to leap over the bed and jump his bones. The knowledge that he'd been deliberately trying to torment her—mission accomplished!—hadn't stopped her traitorous body from responding. She'd gotten so turned on that she'd started climaxing even before he left the room, and long after he'd dropped her off at home, her legs were still shaking. The erotic sight of Michael pleasuring himself had been added to a growing collection of images that were permanently seared into Reese's brain.

"So what happened at the audition?" Raina asked eagerly. "Obviously you guys must have patched things up, or you wouldn't have been chosen as his apprentice."

Smiling, Reese opened her mouth to tell her sister about the wacky audition performance that had landed her a spot on Michael's show.

An hour later, she'd told Raina *everything*. About their wonderful day of sightseeing together, about meeting his family, about watching Michael in his element at the restaurant. Raina listened in rapt absorption, occasionally interrupting for clarification, laughing at funny anecdotes like their paintball adventure, groaning at their heated fight over Victor's roses, sighing poignantly at Michael's romantic overtures and purring wickedly as Reese described—sparingly but honestly—the explosive night of passion they'd shared.

"Oh my God," Raina breathed when Reese had finished speaking. She sounded completely flabbergasted. "I don't even know where to begin. I can't believe how much has happened, and you've barely been there a *week!*"

"I know." Reese sighed.

"If you were the type to play practical jokes, I wouldn't believe any of this. It's so incredible!"

"I'm having a hard time believing it myself. It's been a pretty surreal experience."

"Oh, Reesey." Her sister's voice softened. "Are you…falling in love with Michael?"

Reese choked out a husky laugh that felt like a sob. "According to you and everyone else, I've been in love with him for years."

Raina didn't laugh. "You know what I mean."

Reese closed her eyes as tears crowded her throat, making it ache. "I don't know," she whispered.

Raina was silent for a long moment. "What are you going to do about Victor?"

Reese swallowed with difficulty. "I haven't decided."

"Well, you'd better decide soon," her sister gently advised. "Because when he tunes in to Michael's show on Monday and sees the two of you together, he's going to realize that he's already lost you."

Chapter 15

"Nervous?"

Reese cut a sideways glance at Michael, who stood beside her in the backstage tunnel leading to the set of his show. "What do *you* think?"

He grinned, unfazed by her rancor.

The more relaxed he seemed, the tighter her stomach knotted until she was one big ball of nerves, sweaty palms and a galloping heartbeat. She'd expected *some* stage fright when the big day approached, but this was ridiculous. She hadn't been this nervous since her days of doing clinicals as an intern. Her anxiety that morning was further exacerbated by the growing rumble of crowd noise as the studio audience awaited their entrance. She thought there had to be at least a thousand people out there. She was afraid to ask.

"I think I'm going to be sick," she announced in a thin voice.

Michael chuckled. "That should make for good ratings. My new apprentice, puking all over the set of my kitchen. Nice."

Reese closed her eyes, trying to concentrate on deep-breathing exercises. A moment later her eyes snapped open, and she stared at Michael in fascinated disbelief.

"Are they...*chanting* your name?"

"I believe so." He winked at her. "I much prefer it when you do it, though."

Reese blushed at the reference to the way she'd panted, chanted and screamed his name during sex. Though she'd been trying for days not to think about their lovemaking, she was grateful to him for taking her mind off her jittery nerves, if only for a few moments.

"Only you would think about *that* at a time like this," she grumbled.

His lips curved in a rakish grin. "Food and sex," he drawled. "A match made in heaven."

She blushed harder.

The assistant producer, standing nearby, began his countdown.

Reese tensed up again.

Michael reached out and took her hand, his warm touch infusing her with the strength and courage she needed to get through the next hour.

"Just relax and be yourself," he murmured. "They're going to love you."

She gave him a tremulous smile. "How do *you* know?"

Something softened in his gaze. "Because I—"

"And we're on!"

At the producer's cue Michael slowly released her hand, whispered, "See you soon," then strode out to the set to a deafening chorus of cheers and applause.

Reese watched, mesmerized, as he waved to the audience and shook hands with his band members and several random people in the first row. After kissing his mother, Asha and Samara on the cheek, he made his way onto the stage.

A woman yelled out, "I love you, Michael!"

He grinned and blew her a kiss as laughter and catcalls rippled through the crowd. When a rowdy group of fraternity brothers barked in rapid succession, Michael cupped his hands around his mouth and barked back.

It was, Reese marveled, quite a sight to behold.

When the noise had finally subsided, Michael laid his hand over his heart in a gesture of utmost gratitude. "Thank you so much for that warm Southern welcome. I'm definitely feeling the love right now."

"We missed you, Michael!" This came from a different woman.

He laughed. "I missed y'all, too. It's great to be back for a fourth season of *Howlin' Good,* and I thank all of you for being here and for tuning in at home. Before we get started, how about another round of applause for my family?"

The audience clapped heartily as Sterling, Asha, Celeste, Grant, Marcus and Samara beamed with pleasure.

After acknowledging a few more special guests, Michael continued his introduction. "We've got a lot of exciting things on tap for you this season. But what I'm most excited about is the newest addition to our *Howlin' Good* family. As you all know, this year we launched a nationwide search for an apprentice. I want to thank everyone who submitted your best recipes to us. We had so many amazing, creative dishes to choose from. But at the end of the day, a clear winner emerged, and when you meet her, I think you'll understand why. So without further ado, I'd like to introduce you to my new apprentice, the beautiful and talented Reese St. James."

Reese unglued her leaden feet from the floor and strolled out to the set as she was showered with applause and whistles. Bravely she smiled and waved, inwardly gulping as she took in the size of the studio audience.

As she approached Michael, their eyes met. Suddenly Reese forgot where she was, what she was doing and how she'd even gotten there. No man had *ever* looked at her the way Michael was looking at her now. It was indescribable, a look that drove everything else into the background until he alone was the focus of her attention. The focus of her universe.

This time when her stomach clenched and her pulse quickened, she knew it had nothing to do with stage fright.

As she joined him at the large center island, he gave her an intimate smile that melted her insides faster than a pat of butter tossed into a hot skillet. *What is he trying to do to me?*

"Reese comes to us from Houston," Michael announced, turning to address the audience. "We got any other Houstonians in the house?"

In response to the enthusiastic smattering of cheers, Reese grinned and pumped her fist in solidarity, which drew some appreciative laughter.

"Reese is a doctor," Michael continued with a lazy smile, "but she's taking time out of her busy schedule to study under her favorite chef."

"That's right, Michael," Reese said with just the right touch of breathlessness. "You're my *favorite* chef in the whole—" She broke off suddenly. "What's wrong?"

Michael was frowning down at her white chef's jacket, which had been monogrammed with RSJ—her initials.

"Uh, Reese?"

"Yes, Michael?"

"This *is* my show, right?"

She blinked innocently. "Of course."

"So…why are you wearing *your* initials instead of mine?"

With a sheepish grin, she eased her hand over the embroidered letters. "Oops?"

Michael scowled, shaking his head at the audience. "So much for being *her* favorite chef."

As the crowd roared with laughter, Reese and Michael exchanged sly winks.

"There you are!"

Reese turned and smiled as Celeste and Grant approached her, both elegantly dressed in dark evening wear.

"You and Michael were simply amazing today," Celeste

exclaimed, clasping both of Reese's hands in hers. "I always watch my son's show and thoroughly enjoy it, but that was one of the most entertaining episodes I've ever seen."

Reese warmed with pleasure, though she'd been receiving similar compliments all evening. "Thank you, Mrs. Rutherford. I'm so glad you enjoyed the show." She grinned ruefully, confiding, "I was a nervous wreck."

"No one could tell," Celeste assured her. "You were a natural."

"My wife is right," Grant said, smiling affably at Reese. "If you were anything *but* a physician, I'd encourage you to go into show business."

"Didn't I see Michael's talent agent speaking to you during dinner?" Celeste asked.

Reese laughed. "He gave me his business card and urged me to call him if I ever grow tired of delivering screaming babies for a living—his words, not mine."

Celeste and Grant laughed.

"And speaking of show business," Celeste said, giving Reese an admiring once-over, "you look stunning enough to belong on a red carpet."

Reese beamed. "Thank you very much."

Outfitted in one of Asha's exclusive designs, Reese had never felt more glamorous in her life. Wanting to accentuate Reese's figure, Asha had chosen for her a sleeveless white dress that molded her full breasts, hugged her narrow waist, glided over the curves of her hips and thighs, and ended in a frothy swirl around her feet. It was a sexy, sophisticated ensemble that reminded Reese of something worn by silent-era Hollywood stars. To complete the effect, Asha's stylist had pulled her hair back and arranged it into a simple but elegant twist, while the makeup artist had applied smoky eye shadow and slicked her mouth with a moist red lipstick.

When they'd finished, Asha had taken one look at Reese and sighed. "Darling, you're a vision." While Reese twirled in front of the full-length mirror, Asha had murmured under her breath, "If this doesn't do the trick, nothing will."

"Everyone has been buzzing about today's show," Celeste said, breaking into Reese's musings. "If I didn't know better, I would think it was Michael's, not Asha's party." The satisfied gleam in her eyes made it clear what she thought of *anyone* stealing Asha's spotlight.

After everything Asha had done for Reese, she would have felt guilty taking sides against her. And she didn't necessarily agree with Celeste's assessment, anyway.

But one thing every attendee could agree upon that night: both Michael and Asha knew how to throw one hell of a party. Asha had spared no expense, and Michael's catering crew had more than delivered. The food had been lavish and plentiful, wine flowed freely and the decorations were top-notch. The lush garden sparkled with thousands of fairy lights, and piazzas had been specially erected on platforms to represent Asha's new line of Italian-inspired clothing. Tables grouped together invited guests to linger after dinner to enjoy the starlight and the elegant music provided by a five-string quartet.

As Reese surveyed the sea of strangers garbed in glittering attire, she was struck by the presence of celebrities and fashion heavyweights who had turned out en masse to celebrate the opening of Asha's latest boutique. There were editors from *Vogue, Mademoiselle, Essence, Cosmopolitan,* along with some international reporters and members of the local press.

With Samara in tow, Asha circulated among her guests— greeting friends with double-cheek kisses, introducing acquaintances and lightly admonishing reporters who tried to claim an exclusive with her. "The time for interviews is over, *chère,*" she could be heard saying. "Now it's time to play."

She was totally in her element.

And so, apparently, was Michael.

As Reese's gaze traveled reluctantly across the garden, she saw him and Quentin surrounded by—what else?—a group of leggy, gorgeous models. It was easy to see why the women had flocked to the two friends, who were devastatingly handsome in black tuxedos that made nearly every other man present look like penguins in comparison. As Reese watched, one of the runway kittens leaned close to whisper something in Michael's ear. The sight of his slow, lazy smile was like a knife between Reese's ribs.

Between overseeing his catering staff and mingling with the guests, she hadn't expected to see much of Michael that evening. But she hadn't expected him to completely ignore her, either. She was surprised by how hurt she felt. Hurt and angry.

Celeste, who had followed the direction of her gaze, regarded Reese with an expression of gentle maternal sympathy. "Boys will be boys," she quipped in a feeble attempt at humor.

Reese forced a shrug and an aloof smile.

Inwardly she knew she had no right to expect Michael to spend time with her, especially not after the way she'd practically laughed in his face at the mere suggestion of him being boyfriend material. She wasn't trying to be unkind, but he'd reacted angrily, as though he were deeply offended.

After taping their promo commercial on Thursday, he'd rushed off for a lunch date, and that was the last time Reese had seen him—until today. He'd been so good with her that morning, holding her hand and trying to ease her stage fright. And she would never, ever forget the look on his face as he'd watched her walk toward him. How could he look at her that way, with such tenderness and fierce pride, then turn around and treat her like she didn't even exist?

And here you are thinking you *are the expert on giving mixed signals,* her conscience mocked.

"Grant and I are going inside for a while," Celeste told Reese. "Why don't you come with us, get off your feet for a bit?"

Reese thought of the separate party that was going on inside the main house, where several guests had gathered in the spacious living room to watch the season premiere of *Howlin' Good.* The last thing she needed was a reminder of how much chemistry she and Michael shared.

"That's okay," she said, flashing a bright smile at Celeste. "I'm fine out here. In fact, I think I'll go find Samara. She begged me to rescue her from her mother's clutches at some point this evening."

Celeste looked unconvinced, but she smiled and allowed herself to be led away by Grant.

As Reese started across the garden, she snagged a flute of champagne from a tray carried by a white-gloved waiter. She sipped, smiling when she spied Marcus leading Samara onto the empty dance floor. If anyone could rescue Samara from Asha, it was her husband.

Ignoring the interested stares of several men she passed, Reese found an empty table and sat down.

"Hey, beautiful."

She glanced up, surprised to find Quentin towering over her, his bright hazel eyes twinkling with that irrepressible mischief she remembered so well. She smiled. "Hey, yourself."

"Mind if I join you?"

"Not at all." Reese wondered if any female with functioning X chromosomes ever refused Quentin Reddick.

He folded his long body into a chair and stretched out his endless legs. "Having a good time?"

Reese grinned. "Not as good a time as *you* were obviously having with Asha's models."

He chuckled lazily. "Blame it on my personal motto."

"Which is?"

"Work hard, play even harder."

Reese's grin widened. When she made an exaggerated show of glancing over his broad shoulder, Quentin eyed her curiously.

"What're you looking for?" he asked.

"The string of broken hearts you left in your wake on your way over here."

He laughed, the sound curling around her like a drift of smoke. "I like you."

She fluttered her lashes at him. "Oh, Quentin," she said in a breathy voice. "I bet you say that to *all* the girls."

Again he laughed, shaking his head at her. "Gorgeous *and* sassy. Damn, girl, you are deadly."

"Thanks." Reese grinned, raising her glass in a mock toast before taking a long sip.

A companionable silence lapsed between them as they watched Marcus and Samara swaying together on the dance floor, lost in their own private world.

"It's like being at their wedding again," Quentin murmured.

Reese smiled softly. "I bet it was beautiful. This garden has 'romantic wedding' written all over it."

"It was. Most definitely." He slid a glance at her. "Even Mike cried."

Reese gaped at him. "He *did?*"

Quentin laughed. "Well, he got choked up," he amended, as if he realized he'd violated an unwritten rule of brotherhood: never make your best friend look like a sap to a member of the opposite sex.

"There's nothing wrong with men crying at weddings," Reese remarked. "Especially your brother's wedding. I know how close Michael and Marcus are. I'm sure he was very happy for him."

"Of course," Quentin agreed. "We all were. Especially since no one saw it coming."

"Oh? Did Marcus have commitment issues like his brother?" The moment the words left her mouth, Reese wished she could snatch them back. She'd all but confessed to Quentin that she was falling for his best friend, something she wasn't even ready to admit to herself.

Quentin's eyes narrowed on her face, silently assessing her. After a prolonged moment he nodded slowly, though Reese didn't know whether he was responding to her question or confirming a suspicion about her.

A small, rueful smile touched his mouth. "When we were growing up, there were these two old ladies who used to congregate on their front porch. Every poor neighborhood has them—the nosy old gossips who keep the grapevine going.

Mike's parents' divorce was one of the juiciest scandals to ever hit the block, because of the way things went down. After Mike's mom moved out, every time he and I walked to the corner store, we'd pass those two old ladies. And without fail, we'd hear them cluck their tongues and say to each other—and I quote—'Gonna take a miracle to tame those Wolf boys. Both of them are gonna be heartbreakers. You can thank their mama for that.'"

Reese stared at him. "Every time?"

"*Every* time."

She grimaced and shook her head sympathetically. "That must have been really hard for Michael, having to hear that all the time."

Quentin shrugged. "He got used to it eventually, learned to tune them out. Two years later he was off to college, and poor Marcus had to deal with it. Anyway, you mentioned their commitment issues, so I just wanted to give you some context."

Reese nodded slowly. "What you're telling me is that Michael and Marcus were really scarred by their parents' divorce."

"Yeah," Quentin said quietly. "But I'm not going to get into specifics. I'll let Mike do that."

"What makes you think he's going to confide in me?"

A soft, enigmatic smile curved Quentin's lips. "Call it a hunch."

Reese followed his lazy gaze across the garden to where Michael stood talking to an attractive, fair-skinned woman resplendent in shimmering Chanel. Reese remembered seeing the woman at her audition, and again at today's taping. Whenever they'd made eye contact, Reese had felt as though she were being sized up.

"Who is that woman?" she asked, feigning only casual interest.

The twitch of Quentin's mouth told her that he saw right through her. "That's Andrea Barrister, Mike's publicist."

"No wonder. I've seen her before."

"No surprise there," Quentin drawled ironically. "Wherever you see Mike, Andrea's never too far behind."

Reese felt a pang of jealousy. "I see."

"No, you don't. He's not sleeping with her."

"But you just said—"

"I said that Andrea follows him around everywhere. That doesn't mean they're involved."

"Oh." Reese hesitated, then shrugged dispassionately. "Doesn't matter. It's none of my business."

"No?" Quentin couldn't have conveyed more amused skepticism if he'd tried.

She bristled. "In case you haven't noticed, your friend hasn't said two words to me all evening."

Quentin chuckled. "Aw, hell, girl. He's been watching you the whole night."

"No, he hasn't."

"How would you know?" Those hazel eyes glinted perceptively. "Unless you've been watching him, too?"

Heat stung her face. Averting her gaze, she sipped her champagne.

"You don't believe me? You think I'm lying about him watching you?"

"Yes," Reese said gloomily.

Quentin stood, holding out his hand to her.

She gave him a blank look. "What?"

"Dance with me."

"I don't feel like—"

"Come on, baby girl. You look too damn good to be sitting around moping."

"I'm not—"

But Quentin had already tugged her to her feet and started toward the dance floor.

When Michael glanced up from conversing with his publicist to see Quentin leading Reese onto the dance floor, his first instinct was to storm across the garden and smash his fist into Quentin's face. It took every shred of self-control he possessed to remain where he was, to keep his distance from Reese as he'd been doing all night.

He'd spent the past few days force-feeding himself a litany of reasons why the two of them shouldn't be together. She lived too far away. He didn't do long-distance relationships, so one of them would have to relocate, and he honestly didn't think he was ready to make that kind of sacrifice. Besides, with their busy careers, how much quality time would they really spend together, anyway?

And, of course, there was the matter of her boyfriend. Michael was superstitious enough to believe that if he got Reese by taking her from another man, their relationship might be doomed forever.

But one look at her that morning, and all those rationales—excuses—had gone right out the window. One smile from her, and he'd been a goner. Right then and there, as he was about to go onstage before a live studio audience, he'd looked into Reese's eyes and made the most stunning discovery of his life: he was in love with her.

After that, everything else had been a blur. He was so shaken, so distracted, that it was a miracle he hadn't burned down his kitchen during the taping. Hours later he was still rattled, to the extent that he'd avoided contact with Reese for the entire evening. But he'd seen her. *Oh,* how he'd seen her. He couldn't take his eyes off her in that slinky white siren's dress that hugged every dangerous curve. The first time she turned around, he'd gotten a mind-blowing glimpse of smooth bare skin revealed by the dress's plunging backline. His eyes had bulged, and he'd nearly swallowed his damn tongue. As she'd wafted through the moonlit garden, looking like a heavenly creature, more than a few men had craned their necks to stare and lust after her. Michael had been on edge all night, dreading the inevitable moment when some asshole would make a move on her.

Little did he know it would be his best friend.

Michael glared as Quentin and Reese swayed to the soft, dreamy music. When Quentin leaned down to murmur something in her ear, Michael felt a snarl curling up the corners of his mouth. When Reese tossed back her head and laughed, a red haze settled over his vision. He told himself that Marcus must have forgotten to pass along his warning to Quentin to stay away from Reese. Why else would Quentin risk life and limb by holding her in his arms, putting his hands on her bare back and—

Michael cut Andrea off midsentence. "Excuse me."

He must have resembled a charging bull as he bore down on the dancing couple. He reached them in a matter of seconds and ground out tersely, "Mind if I cut in?"

They glanced around in surprise. Well, *Reese* looked surprised. Quentin looked smug, the bastard.

Quentin slid a lazy glance at Reese. "What do you say, beautiful?" he drawled, his eyes glinting with wicked mischief. "Can my boy have this dance?"

Reese hesitated, biting her lip. When she nodded, Michael felt as relieved as a death row inmate who'd been granted an eleventh-hour gubernatorial pardon.

Quentin grinned, slow and knowing. "I'm gonna go find Lexi. You kids have fun." Winking at them, he strolled off.

Holding Reese's gaze, Michael drew her into his embrace. After a slight hesitation, she rested her head on his shoulder and wreathed her arms around his neck. A shudder rippled through him at the feel of her soft breasts pressed against his chest, her belly to his groin. She was a perfect fit, her body molded to his as if she'd been expressly created for him. The way he felt about her, he wasn't so sure she *hadn't* been.

They began moving together, flowing into an easy rhythm that seemed innate. Like their lovemaking.

Michael tightened his hands around her waist, tilting her closer to him. Her round, curvy butt tempted him beneath the clinging silk of her dress.

"You look breathtaking," he said huskily.

"Thank you," she murmured. "I'm wearing one of Asha's designs."

God bless that woman, Michael thought. "It's incredible."

"I think so, too." Reese paused. "At first I was afraid it might be too—"

"Revealing?"

She chuckled softly. "Yes."

"Now that you mention it, you *have* been getting one too many lewd stares for my liking."

She lifted her head from his shoulder, her eyes glittering with accusation in the silvery moonlight. "You haven't glanced my way all night. How would *you* know how many stares I've been getting?"

He held her gaze. "Sweetheart, I haven't been able to take my eyes off you. If you don't believe me, just ask anyone who's tried to hold a conversation with me tonight."

He could tell that pleased her. She smiled softly, her lush lips glistening like moist, ripe cherries.

Michael wanted to kiss her, but he didn't trust himself to stop there. Not when he was dying to peel off her dress and feast on her voluptuous body, starting with the plump, luscious breasts rubbing against his chest.

Before he succumbed to temptation, he cupped her nape and gently urged her head back to his shoulder. As they continued swaying together, he slanted his head and nuzzled his face against the warm skin of her neck, savoring the light, exotic scent of her perfume. When his hands slid over the silky curve of her back, she shivered.

But he didn't try to do more. Closing his eyes, he simply basked in the rightness of holding her in his arms, where she belonged.

They danced under the stars, so absorbed in each other that time ceased to have meaning.

It was only when Reese whispered, "The music's stopped," that Michael remembered where they were, remembered that they weren't alone.

With obvious reluctance he released her and stepped back.

Lifting his head, he met the knowing gazes of his father and Asha, Marcus and Samara, and Quentin and Lexi, who'd gathered at the edge of the dance floor to watch them. The quiet, intuitive smiles on their faces told Michael that they'd figured out his secret.

Now only one question remained: What was he going to do about it?

It was after 3:00 a.m. by the time the cleanup crew finished their work and departed. After seeing them off, Michael returned to the backyard for a final inspection. Since his father had been generous enough to allow his home to be commandeered by Asha, Michael had given Sterling his word that everything would be restored to perfect order after the party.

After walking the landscaped grounds and satisfying himself that his father would find nothing to complain about, Michael started back toward the house. As he reached the veranda, he caught a flash of movement out of the corner of his eye. He turned, his pulse thudding when he saw Reese's shadowy silhouette in the gazebo.

He started down the flagstone path, strolling at a leisurely pace when all he really wanted to do was run to her like the lovesick fool he was. To distract himself, he admired the gazebo that was painted white with a redbrick roof to match the main house. Surrounded by lush garden beds and draped with a twinkling canopy of fairy lights, it was the perfect spot for a romantic rendezvous.

When he reached it, he found Reese lounging on the wraparound bench, her head tucked into her hand and her legs curled under her. Her feet were bare; the ice-pick stilettos she'd worn earlier now lay on the floor. Michael was pleased to see that she hadn't changed out of the siren's dress, though something would have to be done about her pinned-up hair.

All in good time.

Leaning in the entrance to the gazebo, he dipped his hands into his pockets and gazed at her. "It's late."

"I know."

"Couldn't sleep?"

"Haven't tried."

"Why not?"

Those sultry eyes held his. "I was waiting for you."

His heart went into overdrive.

She sat up slowly, patting the bench beside her. "Come. Sit."

He didn't have to be told twice.

He'd barely sat down before she reached for his tuxedo jacket and began dragging it off his shoulders. He helped her, shrugging out of the jacket and tossing it to the floor.

"Take off your shirt." Her voice was calm.

His was not when he asked, "Why?"

"I want to give you a massage." She smiled. "I think you've earned one."

Michael wasn't about to argue. Hurriedly he unbuttoned his shirt, removed his cuff links and cast them aside with no regard to where they landed.

When Reese's warm fingers settled over his bare skin, he groaned and closed his eyes.

"Look at all these knots you have," she crooned, massaging the cramped muscles. "You poor baby."

"It's been a long day," he mumbled, his head falling limply forward.

"Of course. And you've been working so hard." Her soft, firm hands moved over his shoulders and back, locating and kneading pressure points until he thought he'd melt into a puddle.

"You amaze me, Michael," she murmured. "A man in your position can just sit back and let the people you've hired do all the work. I certainly can't imagine any other celebrity chef helping with kitchen duty at his restaurant, especially after a long, grueling day."

"How do you know…" Michael's brain felt so sluggish he had to stop and try again. "How do you know I didn't do that because *you* were helping?"

She chuckled. "Because one of your waitresses told me you always pitch in. That's one of the many things they admire and respect about you. You never hesitate to get in the trenches with your soldiers."

And speaking of his "soldiers," as the heat of her fingertips sent currents of electric sensation sizzling through his veins, need throbbed heavily in his groin. Before Michael knew it, he had a monster of an erection.

He let out another deep, satisfied groan as her skilled fingers worked at a stubborn knot in his back. "*God,* that feels good. Where'd you learn how to give such incredible massages?"

"My sister taught me. She owns a day spa."

"Yeah?" Michael smiled hazily. "I have a friend whose wife runs a day spa. What's your sister's called?"

"Touch of Heaven."

"Hmm." Something clicked in his lethargic brain. His eyes flew open, and he swung his head around to stare at Reese. "Wait a minute. St. James… Is your sister married to Warrick Mayne?"

Reese smiled. "Yes, she is."

"Get outta here! Are you serious?"

"As a heart attack."

"What a small world," Michael marveled, shaking his head in disbelief. "Warrick and I have known each other for years."

"I know. I just found out the other day when I spoke to my sister."

"Raina, right?"

"Right." Reese shifted, her soft breasts grazing his shoulder as she resumed massaging him. "Apparently, Raina and Warrick were planning to surprise me when you showed up at their wedding. But *you* ruined everything by being a no-show," she said, giving him a teasing poke in the back.

Michael grinned ruefully. "I was really bummed about that. But I'd already committed to judging a competition months before I received their wedding invitation."

"Too bad." She sighed. "We could have met sooner."

He gazed at her. "Better late than never," he said softly.

She met his eyes, her hands stilling on his shoulders. "Michael—"

He leaned close and kissed her. Hard. He didn't know what she'd been about to say. He wasn't taking any chances. He wanted her, needed her more than his next breath, and he wasn't about to give her a chance to tell him no.

She responded hungrily, her arms banding around his neck. Her warm, fruity taste filled his mouth as his tongue invaded hers.

He was desperate for her, but he held it in check, trying to express with his kiss everything that words couldn't describe. He told her with his lips, with every stroke of his tongue, just how much she meant to him, how lost he'd be without her. And she kissed him back with enough fervor to scorch the breath in his lungs.

He worked her dress up her luscious thighs, then lifted her onto his lap. Her legs straddled him on the bench. As he seized her mouth again in a hot, demanding kiss, he reached up and tugged at the band securing her elaborate twist. When she shook her hair free he groaned in approval, sifting his fingers through the dark, silky tresses.

Her hands roamed eagerly over his bare chest, the teasing brush of her fingers making his nipples harden. When she leaned down and flicked her wet tongue over one, then the other, a hard shudder swept through him.

Greedily he cupped her breasts. She gasped and arched into his hands, her taut nipples poking into his palms. He caressed her as her soft, throaty cries ratcheted up his need. She looked like a goddess in her white dress, which glowed in the moonlight and gave her an ethereal sensuality. Last time he'd just wanted to rip off her clothes and feast on her glorious nudity—and later he would. But for now, he was enjoying the erotic vision she made with the tops of her breasts spilling out over the low neckline, her nipples jutting through the silk. It was a dress made for sex.

When she reached behind her to unfasten it, he stopped her. "Keep it on," he whispered thickly. "I wanna make love to you wearing it."

She moaned and undulated against him.

Sliding his hands under her dress, he groaned at the discovery that she wore a silk thong. He cupped her lush, curvy butt and let out another appreciative rumble. "I've been dying to get under here all night."

"It took you long enough," she murmured, making his erection throb.

His hands snaked between her trembling thighs. He pushed aside the damp strip of silk shielding her sex and slid one finger inside. She bucked, her muscles clamping around him. She mewled as he slid his finger in and out of her wetness, pressing and probing. When he found the spongy little spot at the back of her vagina, he tweaked it, then curved his finger forward.

Bingo.

Her eyes flew wide, and he crushed his mouth to hers to muffle her loud cry.

She rode out the orgasm, her thighs shaking on his lap, her fingers digging so hard into his shoulders he knew she'd leave scratches.

Gradually her eyes opened and settled on his face. She stared at him, looking both stunned and fascinated. "No man has *ever* found my G-spot before," she whispered.

His chest swelled. Even in the heat of passion, his male ego wasn't immune to being stroked. "Maybe you've been with the wrong men," he murmured, nibbling her plush lower lip.

She let out a slow, shaky breath. "Maybe."

No maybe *about it,* Michael thought.

Closing her eyes, Reese kissed him softly while her hand reached between their bodies and cupped his erection. She stroked him, wringing a groan from deep in his throat.

She unzipped his fly, reached inside and grasped his engorged shaft. "Mmm," she purred in throaty delight. His penis swelled even more, if that were possible.

"I want to taste you," she murmured seductively.

Pulse hammering, Michael stared in heavy-lidded arousal as she slid off his lap with a soft swish of silk. Holding his gaze, she knelt between his legs, gripped his shaft and took him deep into her mouth. He sucked in a sharp breath. His head fell back and his eyes rolled closed.

"Watch me, Michael," she commanded in that sexy, throaty voice. "I want to see your face while I pleasure you."

He groaned, and nearly came right then and there.

His gaze returned to her luscious, suckling mouth, watching as she licked around and over the head of his penis, then up and down the whole length of him until he was slippery. His eyes slitted in ecstasy. He'd received many enjoyable blow jobs in his life, but he couldn't remember any other woman giving him such excruciatingly intense pleasure.

He swore gutturally as Reese's hot mouth clutched and pulled at him, her tongue swirling sensually before sucking him into another long, gliding caress.

He couldn't take it anymore.

She lifted her head as he dug into his pocket and impatiently yanked out his wallet. He retrieved a condom and fitted it over himself with unsteady hands, then tossed the wallet aside and reached for her.

She stood and straddled his legs, lowering herself onto his lap. At the first touch of his erection she gasped.

Michael's whole body shook with the fierce, primal urge to drive himself deep inside her, to take her quickly and savagely. But he resisted, nudging the head of his shaft up and down her cleft in a slow, controlled caress that defied the lust rampaging through his body.

Her hips pulsed eagerly against him, but he gripped her and held her still. He suckled her lower lip as he circled his penis around her clit, making her squirm and whimper until they were both sure that she wanted this as much as he did. He wanted there to be absolutely no doubt, no room for denials later.

"Do you want me, sweetheart?" he whispered huskily.

"You know I do," she panted, her eyes glazed with desire.

He slid his tongue into her mouth, imitating the shallow, teasing thrusts he was making with his hips. "Then say it, Reese. Say you want me."

She choked out a frustrated sob. "Why are you—"

"*Say it.*"

"I want you, Michael. I want you. *Want* you."

He smiled with dark triumph. "Good. Then you can have me."

He thrust himself inside her with one deep, hard lunge and captured her mouth to swallow her scream.

She clutched his shoulders and rocked her hips against him as he began pumping into her. But they were both already so aroused that a few hard thrusts later, they exploded.

Reese flung back her head, her muscles contracting around him as he closed his eyes and groaned harshly.

They clung to each other for a long time, his hands stroking the silky warmth of her back as he murmured endearments to her.

At length she lifted her head from his shoulder and gazed into his eyes with searching tenderness. His heart constricted. He leaned close, kissing her deeply and possessively.

She belonged to him now.

And nothing or no one would stop him from claiming what was rightfully his.

Inside the cozy guesthouse located on the opposite end of the gazebo, Asha lay curled against Sterling's side in the large bed where they'd just finished making love.

"Do you think anyone suspects anything?"

Sterling chuckled, a drowsy rumble. "About us? Or about Michael and Reese?"

"About us, of course." Asha laughed softly. "Darling, everyone who was at the party tonight knows about Michael and Reese, not to mention the millions of viewers who tuned in to watch his show. My God, Sterling. Did you see the way he looked at her?"

"See it? Hell, I *felt* it."

Sterling had never seen his son look at any woman the way he'd looked at Reese St. James. And they must have stayed on that empty dance floor for over an hour. If the musicians hadn't stopped for a break, there was no telling how much longer those two would have danced together, oblivious to everything else.

Sterling wanted Michael to be happy, and Reese, God bless her, seemed to be just what the doctor ordered—no pun intended.

Asha sighed blissfully. "Looks like we'll be planning another wedding in the garden soon."

"We?"

"Of course. We both know you can't be trusted to help plan a wedding. For starters, we already know what you'd include on the reception menu."

Sterling scowled without rancor. "Michael happens to love barbecue. He's been grilling since he was ten years old."

"He's a world-renowned chef," Asha said drily. "He can't serve pork ribs and beans at his own wedding. And Reese is a doctor—"

"From Texas, another barbecue-loving state."

"—who'd expect nothing less than a classy wedding."

Sterling guffawed. "Classy, hell. Reese is one of the most down-to-earth girls Michael has ever brought home."

"Are you saying she's not classy?" Asha challenged.

"Of course not. She's got more class in her pinky finger than most people I know. But she's not fussy or pretentious. She's genuine. I think that's one of the many qualities my son loves about her."

"It doesn't hurt that she's exquisite. That body." Asha sighed. "I'm already looking forward to designing her wedding gown."

Sterling smiled softly. "Watching her and Michael on that dance floor—him in a tux and her dressed in white—it felt like we were already at their wedding."

"I know." Something in Asha's quiet, triumphant voice made Sterling wonder if she'd orchestrated the whole thing. It wouldn't surprise him. The woman was a damn control freak.

As if to prove his point, she said, "They can honeymoon at my chateau in France."

Unnerved by the decisive finality in her tone, as if the matter were a foregone conclusion, Sterling muttered, "Michael has a cottage in Italy. I'm sure they'd want to honeymoon there instead."

"Of course. How romantic."

Asha's casual mention of her French chateau was just another reminder of the vastly different worlds she and Sterling inhabited, as illustrated by tonight's glitzy bash. Gussied up in an Armani tux, with a champagne flute held awkwardly in his hand, Sterling had felt out of place as Asha led him around the garden, introducing him to her snooty friends. Between the French and the couture lingo, Sterling had had a hard time following any conversation. He'd finally given up and retreated to the house to hang out with the normal folks from Michael's television studio.

He didn't belong in Asha's world, and he never would.

This thing between them—whatever it was—would fizzle out as soon as she returned to her glamorous, fast-paced life in New York. If being a cop hadn't been good enough for Celeste, being a *retired* cop definitely wouldn't be good enough for the likes of Asha Dubois. Sure, Sterling's circumstances were much different now than they'd been during his marriage. He was well provided for by his sons, who gave him a generous monthly stipend and saw to it that he never wanted for anything. Hell, if he'd been a greedy, materialistic man, Michael and Marcus would've had him living larger than Donald Trump, with vacation properties and luxury cars galore. Those boys loved to spoil their old man, and they made no apologies for it.

But all the money in the world couldn't buy a woman like Asha.

After finding herself pregnant and divorced by the age of nineteen, she'd become as jaded about romance as Sterling was. Although she'd been romantically linked to several tycoons over the years, she'd made it perfectly clear that she had no interest in shackling herself to another man.

Sterling had no illusions about their future.

They *had* no future.

But that didn't stop him from wanting her in his bed. They'd been sneaking around for the past week, having the kind of sex that could put a man his age in the hospital. Asha was a sensual, passionate lover who knew how to satisfy a man's every need. She was also a screamer, which was why they'd relocated their nightly trysts to the guesthouse.

Sterling was so addicted to her that he'd even invited her to accompany him and the family on a relaxing five-day getaway to Sea Island, a luxury golf resort off the coast of Georgia. He'd been thrilled—and shocked—when Asha had agreed to go. Now that her boutique was open and the party was over, there was nothing keeping her in Atlanta. He knew she had pressing matters awaiting her in New York. Her cell phone rang constantly, and she'd frequently been overheard fretting about preparations for her upcoming fall collection. But for whatever reason, she'd decided to extend her stay in Atlanta. And Sterling—to his detriment—couldn't be happier.

"You never did answer my question."

Pulled out of his reverie, Sterling gazed down at Asha. "What question was that?"

"Forgot already?"

He chuckled. "I'm old, remember?"

"Mmm," she purred, snaking a satiny thigh between his legs. "I beg to differ."

Sterling's heart thudded. Another night with this woman,

and he'd need a damn pacemaker. "Oh, that's right. You asked me if I think anyone suspects that we're sleeping together."

"We haven't actually done much sleeping," Asha pointed out.

Sterling gulped. "I don't think my boys suspect anything, or they would've called me out already." He thought fleetingly of Celeste, who'd been even more hostile to Asha than usual, for reasons unknown. "What about Samara? Has she said anything to you?"

Asha smiled against his chest. "I've caught her giving me strange looks every now and then. And I think she was a little suspicious when I told her I'd decided to stay here instead of her house. But I just explained to her that it made more sense for me to be here to meet with the caterers and to finalize preparations for the party. And since we're all leaving for the coast tomorrow, I don't have to worry about coming up with another excuse for why I'm still sleeping at your house."

Sterling grinned. "Sounds like you've thought of everything."

"Mmm-hmm." Her thigh slid higher. "Wanna hear what I'm thinking now?"

"Why don't you just *show* me?" Sterling suggested, rolling her onto her back.

She laughed, her arms going around his neck. As he lowered his head to kiss her, she interjected, "Oh, but wait. Aren't you the one who just said you're old?"

He flashed a rakish smile. "I'm old, honey. Not dead."

Chapter 16

Reese knew what she had to do.

She'd been putting off the inevitable for days, possibly even months. But everything had changed now, and she could no longer run from the truth: she and Victor were over. So there was only one thing left for her to do. She had to end their relationship.

She'd spent the day rehearsing what she would say to him. But when she called him that night, she had to settle for leaving a message on his voice mail: "Victor, this is Reese. We need to talk. Please call me."

When the phone rang an hour later, she assumed it was Victor and instinctively braced herself as she answered, "Hello?"

"Hey."

It was him. The man who'd infiltrated her defenses and stolen her heart, a heart she'd been unable to surrender to Victor. Because she'd been secretly saving it for *him*.

"Hi," she said shyly.

"I miss you," Michael said in that deep, intoxicating voice that was impossible to resist. "I want to see you."

A wave of pleasure washed over her. A soft smile curved her lips as she leaned back against the headboard and closed her eyes. "You just saw me, what, five hours ago? We spent half the day together, remember?"

"Half isn't good enough," he growled.

Her smile widened. "Aren't *you* greedy?"

"When it comes to you, sweetheart, I want it all."

Her heart turned over. She wondered if he knew what he was saying. She was afraid to hope. "I miss you, too," she whispered.

"So why are we doing all this missing when there's a simple remedy?"

"I don't know." Struck by a sudden suspicion, she asked, "Where are you, Michael?"

"Standing on your doorstep."

She was already on her feet, her pulse racing with excitement as she rushed through the living room to reach the front door. Hurriedly she unlocked it and yanked it open.

And there he was.

Dressed in a black T-shirt and black jeans, his midnight eyes glittering in the soft glow of the porch light.

They stared at each other, still holding their cell phones.

"Hi." Reese felt as giddy as a teenager in the throes of her first major crush.

Michael tucked his phone into his back pocket. Without a word, he scooped an arm around her waist and slanted his mouth over hers in a deep, drugging kiss that left her weak-kneed and breathless.

"Mmm," he murmured, gently suckling her lower lip. "That's an excellent cabernet."

Reese smiled dreamily. "Wow. You're good." Before calling Victor, she'd drank a glass of wine to calm her nerves.

Michael drew away, mouth twitching as he took her phone from her ear and handed it to her. Reese laughed, embarrassed because she'd forgotten she was still holding it.

His gaze raked over her, taking in her red tube top and denim skirt. "Good, you're still dressed."

"Why?"

"I thought we could grab a bite to eat."

"*Now?* But it's after eight o'clock."

He grinned. "And your point is?"

"Well, it's kind of late to be eating dinner. And after all that food they served us at the studio luncheon, I'm not even sure I have room for anything else."

"So we'll eat something light," Michael proposed.

Reese was skeptical. "Something light, huh? I don't even want to *think* about how much weight I've gained since meeting you, Michael."

He gave her another slow, appreciative once-over. "You definitely won't hear me complaining."

She laughed. "That's because *you're* not the one gaining weight!"

But he was already turning her by the shoulders and nudging her in the direction of her bedroom. "Go put some shoes on, woman."

"Okay, okay. Sheesh, you don't have to be so boss— Ow!" she yelped as he smacked her lightly on the butt.

He grinned at her. "There's more where that came from if you don't hurry up."

She stuck her tongue out at him. When he took a threatening step toward her, she scampered off with a squeal.

They went to a gourmet market that specialized in imported meats, cheeses and wines. Holding hands and smiling at each other, they meandered through the aisles, adding various items to their basket. A loaf of crusty bread, a thick wedge of Parmigiano Reggiano cheese, some prosciutto ham and salami. It felt so natural, so *right,* to be shopping with Michael that Reese couldn't help fantasizing that they were already a couple. She imagined them taking weekend trips to the market, then returning home and cooking together, taste-testing each other's food between slow, lazy kisses. When the meal was ready they'd uncork a bottle of wine and dine by candlelight, then spend the rest of the night making love.

The images were so vivid that an ache of longing flooded Reese's heart. It shook her to realize how hard she'd fallen for Michael, and how much she wanted a future with him.

God help her if he didn't feel the same.

When they left the market, he surprised her by heading to his father's house in Stone Mountain.

"I thought we were eating at your place," Reese said, puzzled.

"I changed my mind." He slanted her a glance. "With everyone gone for the rest of the week, we'll have the place all to ourselves."

Reese decided not to point out to him that they would have had privacy at his penthouse, as well. As long as they were together, it didn't matter where they ate.

When they arrived at Sterling's house, she was so engrossed in their conversation about tomorrow's taping of *Howlin' Good* that she didn't notice where they were going until they'd passed under a wood arbor draped in vines and perennials.

And then they were in the garden, and just as with her first visit, Reese felt as if she was stepping into paradise. The eruption of colorful flowers was breathtaking, while tall oaks, Japanese maple and tulip poplar trees arched overhead in a canopy of foliage that added to the lush surroundings. As impressive as last night's decorations had been, nothing compared to the spectacular beauty of the garden in its natural state.

Guided by torchlights, Michael led Reese farther down the winding path until they came upon an arched wooden bridge that overlooked a small pond. There, in a nearby patch of green lawn, was a wicker picnic basket perched upon a red-and-white checkered blanket.

Reese gasped, her startled gaze swinging around to Michael's face. "You did this?"

He smiled. "Surprise."

"Oh my God," she breathed. A picnic in an enchanted, moonlit garden. Talk about romantic!

"When did you...?" She trailed off, speechless.

Michael chuckled. "I came right over after I dropped you off this afternoon," he answered, drawing her down onto the blanket.

Reese gaped at him. "*That's* why you told me you had things to do."

He nodded. "Believe me, sweetheart, I wouldn't have left you if I didn't have every intention of seeing you again."

His words sent a melting warmth rushing through her. She smiled, gazing into his dark eyes and falling harder. "This is... Words can't even describe how wonderful this is, Michael."

His expression softened. He brushed his fingers across her face, then began removing items from the basket. An assortment of luscious fruit, cheeses and pasta salads to complement the foods they'd bought at the market.

Reese smiled as he produced a bottle of Chianti, filled two wineglasses and passed one to her.

"To romantic moonlight picnics," she toasted him.

"And many more," Michael murmured, holding her gaze as they clinked glasses and sipped.

She told herself not to read too much into his words, but it was hard not to when his eyes were filled with such tender promise.

They sat close together on the blanket and fed each other, sharing kisses between bites, drinking from the same glass of wine.

It was the most romantic meal Reese had ever had.

And the most stimulating, she added as she fed Michael a big, juicy grape and watched his lips close around her fingertips. Her nipples tightened, and heat pooled between her legs.

There was a sensual gleam in his eyes as he asked silkily, "Are you ready for dessert?"

"Yes." Her mouth was watering—and that was before she saw the dessert he removed from the basket. A three-layer confection frosted with creamy chocolate ganache and drizzled with fudge and white chocolate.

"Oh my," Reese breathed, watching as he cut a thick slice for her. "What *is* that?"

"My triple chocolate cheesecake." His lips curved. "Or, as I like to call it, chocolate orgasm."

"Have mercy."

As he raised a forkful to her lips, she opened and got a mouthful of molten, decadently rich chocolate. She closed her eyes with a deep moan. "Oh, Michael…"

"Good?"

"Good? This is *sinful.* I can see why you call it chocolate orgasm."

He fed her another bite, his gaze intent on her mouth. "I'm glad you like it," he said, low and husky.

"Like it? I *love* it, Michael. You are truly a chef extraordinaire."

He smiled, sampling a forkful of the gooey delicacy. "Not bad," he murmured, slowly licking the fork. "Not bad at all."

"You and your understatements," Reese whispered, her breasts throbbing as she watched the snakelike motions of his tongue, reliving all the wicked things that tongue had done to her body.

Catching her hungry gaze, Michael forked up another bite of cake and slid it into her mouth, then fed himself a second piece. By the time the plate was empty, their lips were fused in a ravenous, openmouthed kiss, tongues swirling as they shared a delicious kaleidoscope of flavors.

Reese whimpered in protest as Michael abruptly pulled away.

"Shhh," he whispered, brushing his thumb across her lips as he reached inside the wicker basket with the other hand. "There's something I've been dying to do since the night I met you."

"What?" she asked dazedly.

He held up a plastic container of melted chocolate sauce,

his eyes glinting wickedly. "I'm going to pour this all over your body and lick it off."

Reese shivered with arousal, already shimmying out of her denim skirt and panties.

Michael yanked off her tube top, swearing hoarsely when her breasts sprang free. "No bra?"

"Didn't need one," she panted.

He made a guttural sound in his throat. "Lie down," he commanded.

She did as he told her, trembling with desire and anticipation as he swirled his finger in the container. Then, holding her gaze, he smeared both of her areolas with warm chocolate. Reese groaned, watching as he bent his head and slowly, erotically, licked her nipples clean. Spasms of pleasure speared through her loins.

"Mmmm," he murmured against her, the vibration of his deep, rumbling voice ratcheting up her need. "You taste better than anything I've ever tasted in my life."

Her belly quivered. She reached for his hand and drew his finger into her mouth, sucking off the last traces of chocolate. "So do you."

He shuddered, his eyes blazing with fierce arousal. Like an artist creating a masterpiece, he poured several lines of chocolate up and down her trembling stomach. It took Reese a dazed moment to realize that he'd painted an *M* on her.

"*M* is for Michael," he said in that dark, mesmerizing voice, "because you're mine. Now spread your legs for me, sweetheart."

When Reese obeyed, he dribbled chocolate between her thighs, coating the swollen folds of her labia and clitoris. The sensation was like nothing she'd ever felt before. She moaned, loud and long.

"This," Michael murmured, dipping two fingers into her chocolate-drenched sex, "is *definitely* mine."

Reese couldn't have argued even if she'd wanted to. When he withdrew his possessive fingers and slid them into his mouth, she nearly lost her damn mind.

"Michael," she whimpered helplessly. "I'm about to—"

Lowering his head, he captured her mouth in a deep, carnal kiss flavored with chocolate and her own nectar. "Don't come yet," he ordered huskily. "I'm just getting started."

Reese groaned. *Heaven help me!*

Michael drew away and began moving down her body, his tongue tracing the path of the chocolate *M* he'd painted onto her. Reese shook from the inside out. Feeling wanton, she cupped her breasts and tugged at her aching nipples.

And then Michael's mouth was on her sex, sucking, lapping at the melted chocolate sauce. She cried out, writhing against him in mindless ecstasy. The stroking motions of his hot, silky tongue were out of this world. She'd never experienced anything like this with Victor. It seemed only fitting that Michael, her fantasy lover, would be the first man ever to find her G-spot *and* give her a chocolate orgasm.

He tongued her like there was no tomorrow, voraciously licking and sucking, making her body weep. When his tongue plunged inside her and swirled around, Reese bucked and arched into him, pleasure cresting over her like a tidal wave. She screamed as she came, and he drew out her orgasm by gently pulling at her clitoris with his teeth.

She was still trembling violently, eyes closed, when she heard a tear of foil—a sound that was pure music to her ears. There was a rustling of fabric as Michael quickly undressed. A moment later he was embedded fully inside her, stretching her, his arms braced on either side of her head as he thrust furiously into her. Moaning his name, Reese tightened her legs around his waist and crossed her ankles at the small of his back to take him deeper, as deep as he could possibly go.

His beautiful, muscular body glowed in the silvery radiance of the moonlight. A range of raw emotions played across his taut face. Passion, tenderness, reverence. A focused determination to satisfy her every need.

She clung tightly to him, her nails raking his back as she tried to match the relentless pumping of his hips. Her second orgasm hovered just beyond her reach. A few more strokes were all she needed.

But suddenly Michael pulled out of her and growled, "Turn over. I want to take you from behind."

Reese eagerly complied, kneeling on all fours. He loomed behind her, his thick, rigid erection pressed against her bottom. She gasped and arched in surprise as he drizzled chocolate along the length of her spine, then bent forward and licked his way down to the cleft of her buttocks. She groaned, shivering uncontrollably. Closing her eyes, she reached down and stroked her throbbing clitoris, on the verge of climaxing. *Hard.*

His rough hands gripped her bottom, tilting her hips back and positioning her right where he wanted her. And then he thrust high and deep, his heavy body slapping against her backside, jerking a sharp cry out of her throat. She glanced over her shoulder, aroused by the sight of him watching his penis slide into her. The look of savage hunger on his face was another erotic image that would be indelibly etched into her brain.

As she pulsed her hips against him, he groaned. "I'm so addicted to you, Reese. I can't get enough of you."

Her heart swelled at the vulnerability in his voice. It was low and shaky, ragged with desperate longing.

"Tell me what you want, baby," he entreated her. "I'll give you anything. *Anything.*"

Reese couldn't get her throat to work. But it didn't matter. He was already giving her exactly what she wanted, a deep, surging rhythm that stroked every part of her swollen, aching sex. She moaned and rocked against him, clutching fistfuls of the picnic blanket. He cupped her swaying breasts and fondled them, his thumbs rubbing her tight, engorged nipples in a caress that nearly undid her. He had such command of her body, her mind, her soul. No matter what happened between them, she would always, *always* belong to him.

Soon his slow, controlled rhythm changed, and Reese's breath gasped out of her with the force of his voracious, pounding thrusts. She arched her back and frantically worked herself against him, reaching behind her to grip his round, flexing butt. He groaned, grabbing a handful of her hair and winding it around his fingers. He pulled her head back, forcing her to meet the glittering intensity of his gaze.

"I'm never letting you go," he whispered fiercely, biting her neck as if to brand her. "So you'd better tell your boyfriend to get ready for the fight of his damn life."

Reese's heart soared, and she breathlessly confessed, "You don't have to fight. I'm breaking up with him."

Michael's grip gentled on her hair. And then he laughed, a sound of exultant male triumph mingled with unmistakable relief.

Three strokes later he exploded, shouting her name in a hoarse, reverential voice. His rapid, pulsing contractions triggered Reese's own release, and she threw back her head as spasms of bright, white-hot rapture tore through her.

"Michael…Michael…" His name poured out of her in a succession of desperate, keening wails. Tears of joyous wonder welled in her eyes and spilled down her cheeks.

Shuddering and panting hard, Michael curved his arms around her and pulled her down onto the blanket, surrounding her with his warmth. Reese closed her eyes with a deep, satiated sigh and wondered whether it was possible to die from sheer bliss.

They lay spooned together, listening to the gurgling pond and the lazy drone of crickets as the sultry night wrapped around them.

"It's so peaceful out here," Reese whispered, as if she were afraid to shatter the garden's tranquility. "I could stay right here all night."

"Who says you were going anywhere, anyway?" Michael murmured, nuzzling the sweat-dampened hair at her nape.

Warmth tingled through her veins. She sighed. "Sleeping under the stars. How utterly romantic."

"Well, now, I never said anything about sleeping."

She laughed. "You can't keep me up another night, Michael, or I won't be able to function on the set tomorrow."

"You did just fine today," he drawled, his warm breath tickling her as he nibbled her earlobe.

She shivered. "Be that as it may, I still need to get some rest. Back home, I had a nine o'clock bedtime."

He snorted softly. "You might as well forget about that. I usually don't get home from the restaurant until after eleven, and there's no way in hell I'd be able to crawl into bed with you and keep my hands to myself."

A foolish smile spread helplessly across Reese's face. He was talking as if they were already a couple, the very thing she'd been fantasizing about all night. "Then I suggest you start bringing your butt home earlier, Mr. Executive Chef," she sassed.

"Yes, ma'am." But his voice had grown quieter, and the lips that had been nuzzling her suddenly went still.

Silence lapsed between them, punctuated by the crickets' noisy chirping.

As Reese's euphoria faded, she drew a shallow breath. "So...when does your family return?"

"Saturday."

She nodded slowly. "And Asha went with them?"

"Yeah. You sound surprised."

"I guess I am. Once the party was over, I just assumed she'd hop on her private plane and head back to New York. I know how busy she is. Her assistant, Pierre, must have called her a hundred times the day we went shopping together."

"Hmm." Michael paused. "Samara thinks something may be going on between Asha and my father."

"Really?" Reese turned in the cradle of his arms to stare at him. "But they're always bickering."

His amused gaze met hers. "Maybe that's because they're fighting an attraction. You and I know something about that."

She grinned wryly. "Good point."

"Anyway, they haven't been arguing as much as they used

to. So maybe Samara's on to something. She and Marcus are keeping a close eye on them during the trip."

Reese shook her head, marveling, "Your father and Asha. Now *that* would be the ultimate example of opposites attracting." She searched Michael's face. "How would you feel about them hooking up?"

"It'd be a little weird at first," he admitted, smiling. "I can't see my father with a high-maintenance woman like Asha. But if they make each other happy, then I'm all for it. God knows the old man deserves to be happy."

Reese hesitated, then ventured cautiously, "Because of the way things turned out between him and your mother?"

Michael nodded.

Reese held her breath, waiting to see if he would confide in her, as Quentin had so confidently predicted.

Just when she'd started to lose hope, Michael said in a low voice, "When I was sixteen, my mother cheated on Dad with Grant. They worked at the same hospital. She was a nurse, and Grant was a big-shot neurosurgeon. Marcus came home early from school one day and caught them kissing in the kitchen."

Suppressing a horrified gasp, Reese said, "Poor Marcus. He was only—"

"Ten. And to give you an idea of how traumatized he was, it took him twenty-five years to forgive her."

"And you?" Reese gently probed. "How long did it take you?"

"A while." Michael's expression was grim. "After the divorce, she disappeared from our lives for a long time, missed a lot of important things. I think she felt guilty, and that's why she and Grant waited several years to get married. Anyway, when I agreed to give her away at her wedding, we had a long heart-to-heart, and I got to hear her side of the story for the first time."

He blew out a deep breath. "To make a long story short, she'd turned to Dad for consolation one night after her high school sweetheart was killed in a car accident. They slept together, and she wound up getting pregnant. They were both scared and devastated, but being the honorable man he's always been, Dad offered to marry her and raise her child as his own, whether or not I was."

Incredulous, Reese stared at him. "There was a possibility you weren't Sterling's son?"

Michael nodded. "Mom had slept with her boyfriend two nights before he was killed. So, yeah, there was a question about my paternity."

"That seems impossible. You're the spitting image of Sterling. Anyone can see that you're his son."

His mouth curved in a half smile. "And a paternity test proved that I was."

"So you're the reason your parents got married."

He nodded. "And Marcus is the reason they stayed together for as long as they did. As I learned, their marriage was doomed long before Grant entered the picture."

"Because she was still in love with her high school sweetheart," Reese surmised.

"That, and they both felt trapped by their circumstances, forced into a marriage of convenience." Michael paused, bitterness edging his voice as he added, "Though Mom would never admit it to me or Marcus, we both know she resented Dad being a cop. We were poor, and Grant was able to give her the life Dad never could."

"Your father doesn't seem at all resentful," Reese said quietly. "To look at him and your mother, you'd never suspect that she betrayed him."

"Dad has a very big, forgiving heart," Michael said, unmistakable pride in his voice. "As much as he was hurting, he never spoke ill of Mom. He made excuses for her whenever she missed a birthday or an important event in our lives, and he spent years playing peacemaker. In the end I decided that if *he* could forgive her, so could I."

Reese gazed tenderly at him. "I'm glad you did. I don't think anyone should ever underestimate the power of forgiveness."

Michael nodded. His arm had been resting across her waist. Now his thumb traced an idle pattern on her hip.

Reese hesitated, biting her lower lip. "Can I tell you about a crazy suspicion I've had since meeting your parents?"

His thumb stilled. A new guardedness entered his expression. "What?"

"I think it's possible that, uh, your mother might still have feelings for your father. And I think that's why she perceives Asha as a threat."

Michael stared at Reese in a way that made her wish she'd kept her theory to herself. "You're wrong," he said with implacable calm.

"What if I'm not?"

"You are. Mom gave up everything to be with Grant. She's not going to decide, almost thirty years later, that she made a mistake and wants Dad back."

Reese didn't know whether he was trying to convince her or himself. Either way, God help Celeste Rutherford if Reese's suspicions about her were true.

"Anyway," Michael drawled, his teeth sinking delicately into Reese's shoulder, "this is supposed to be a romantic moonlight picnic. Enough about my parents."

Reese cuddled closer, smiling when she felt his penis hardening against her belly. As he began sliding down the length of her body, she purred, "I want another piece of that cake. What'd you call it again?"

"Sweetheart," Michael murmured, sucking her toe into his mouth, "I got your chocolate orgasm right here."

Chapter 17

The next nine days marked nine of the most blissful days of Reese's life.

From the moment she and Michael awoke in the morning until they collapsed into each other's arms at night, they were inseparable. They shopped, planned meals and cooked together. She thoroughly enjoyed working alongside him every day, both on the set of his show and at the restaurant, where he'd taken her under his wing as an unofficial cook. Under his tutelage, Reese was learning a lot about culinary arts and testing her newfound skills on his willing customers, who got a kick out of being served by Michael's sassy apprentice. After a full day of taping and working at the restaurant, they often snuggled in bed together and read e-mails from viewers who couldn't get enough of their on-screen chemistry.

But their sizzling performances didn't stop when the cameras weren't rolling. They'd christened nearly every corner of Michael's penthouse and the restaurant, and had even made love on the set after hours—an erotic, mind-blowing interlude that had them both grinning throughout the next day's taping. They couldn't get enough of each other.

One evening they babysat for Marcus and Samara. The sight of Michael laughing and roughhousing with his nephews filled Reese with such acute longing that she had to leave the room to compose herself.

Unbeknownst to Michael or her family, she'd started looking into positions at several local hospitals. Though she and Michael had yet to say *I love you* to each other, she sensed that it was only a matter of time before he'd be ready to take the next step. Every time their bodies were joined, or they shared a secret glance across a crowded room, she was convinced that the look of tender ferocity in his eyes *had* to be love. But for some reason he was holding back, and Reese was enough of a self-preservationist to wait for him to be the first to utter the magic words.

It turned out to be the wisest decision she'd ever made.

On the Friday before the last taping of the apprentice series, she arrived at the studio after running errands to go over some final preparations with Michael and Drew Corbett. She also had some important news to share with Michael. Layla had just called from Somalia to tell Reese that the funding for her photography assignment had been cut, so she'd be returning home next week. Which meant that once Reese completed her final episode of *Howlin' Good,* she'd have no reason to remain in Atlanta.

Unless she and Michael had a future together.

That afternoon, as she neared the open doorway to Drew's office, she overheard him speaking excitedly to Michael. "…network execs are buzzing about keeping her on as a regular on the show. You know I'm totally on board, but what about you? Or do I even have to ask?"

"What's that supposed to mean?"

"Well, I think it's pretty obvious to everyone that you're crazy about her."

Reese's pulse quickened. She found herself awaiting Michael's response with bated breath.

He chuckled. "She's a ratings magnet. How could I *not* be crazy about her?"

Reese's heart plummeted. As reality came crashing down on her, she realized that everything she and Michael had shared over the past nine days had been a joke.

And the joke was on her.

Somehow she made it through the meeting without betraying her emotions. She laughed at Drew's corny jokes, and interacted with Michael as if he hadn't just plunged a dagger through her heart.

When the meeting was over, she told Michael she had more errands to run and assured him that she would call him once she was finished.

Four hours later, she was on a plane home to Houston.

She knew her decision to skip town had been impulsive, but she had to get away and collect herself, if only for a couple days. She was contractually obligated to return to Atlanta for Monday night's final taping. After that, she'd be free to leave for good—which she intended to do.

Given what she'd overheard that afternoon, what other choice did she have? Michael had all but admitted that she meant nothing more to him beyond what she could do for his show's popularity. And since he'd never had any problem with ratings, that meant he *really* didn't need her.

It was devastating to realize that she'd been living in a fantasy world. But it was better that she'd come to her senses now, *before* she rearranged her entire life for a man who'd never intended to commit to her.

As for the man she'd dated for the past year, hoping to convince herself that they were right for each other, it was time to close that door once and for all.

The morning after she arrived home, she drove to the hospital where she and Victor worked and had him paged. She knew he'd been avoiding her phone calls for over a week. It was time for both of them to face the music.

When he came on the line, she said without preamble, "Victor, this is Reese. I'm sitting outside in a rental car. I don't want to come inside and get sidetracked by my coworkers. I know you don't have any surgeries scheduled this morning. Will you meet me outside so we can talk?"

A heavy pause. "There's not much to talk about, Reese."

"What do you mean?"

"I've watched the show. After you told me about your apprenticeship I was angry, and I didn't plan to watch a single minute. But I'm glad I finally did."

Reese swallowed hard. "Victor—"

"I hope to hell you know what you're doing," he said harshly. "Michael Wolf is a damn celebrity. When he breaks your heart, maybe then you'll realize he wasn't worth what you've given up."

The line went dead.

Reese closed her eyes, grateful, at least, that she'd been spared having to make a long, painful breakup speech.

Chapter 18

Michael paced up and down his living room floor, his cell phone pressed to his ear. "Come on, come on," he muttered under his breath. "Answer the damn phone. Answer the—"

"Hello."

Relief swept through him. "*Reese?* I've been trying to reach you since last night! What the hell are you doing in Houston?"

"I came home for the weekend." She paused. "I guess Drew's assistant told you."

"She did," he snapped. "But why the hell did I have to hear it from her instead of *you?*"

"Don't worry," she said coolly. "I'll be back on Monday to tape the grand finale."

"I don't give a damn about the show!" Michael shouted.

"Really? You were singing a different tune yesterday."

"What are you talking about?"

Reese sighed. "I overheard the comment you made to Drew before our meeting."

"What com—" Suddenly Michael froze, the words echoing

through his mind like a cruel indictment. *She's a ratings magnet. How could I not be crazy about her?*

He'd regretted the careless remark as soon as the words left his mouth. It was a stupid thing to have said, and so far from the truth it was laughable. Except he wasn't laughing now. And neither, apparently, was Reese.

"I didn't mean what I said," he told her. "You know that, don't you?"

"Actually, I think you did." She sounded so calm. Resigned. "I think what you told Drew was more honest than anything you've ever told me."

"What? How can you say that? How can you *believe* that?"

"The question is, how could I have ever believed otherwise?"

Dread coiled in Michael's gut. "Reese, listen to me. I—"

"I'm not angry, Michael," she interrupted in that mild, implacable tone. "Deep down inside, I've always known that our relationship was too good to be true. It's time for me to stop chasing a fantasy and get back to reality."

He scowled. "What the hell is that supposed to mean?"

"It means that I'm returning to Houston after Monday's final taping. Layla's funding got cut, so she'll be home early next week. There's no reason for me to stay in Atlanta."

"What about me?" Michael growled, desperation mingling with anger. "What about us?"

"There *is* no us."

The quiet finality in her voice ripped his heart in half. "Reese, don't—"

"I'll see you on Monday. Goodbye, Michael."

That evening, Sterling was in his den playing poker with Michael and Marcus when Frizell spoke from the window. "Are you expecting company, Mr. Wolf?"

At first he didn't hear the question. He'd been preoccupied with Michael, who'd been brooding ever since he arrived at the house that night. Sterling knew something bad must have happened between his son and Reese, but so far Michael hadn't said a word.

"Mr. Wolf?" Frizell prompted. "Are you expecting company?"

"No." Sterling was still recovering from the departure of his last houseguests. Or rather, from Asha's departure. He hadn't heard a peep from her since she'd returned to New York. Just as he'd expected.

"There's a limo coming down the driveway," Frizell told him.

Suddenly Sterling's nerves tightened and his pulse thudded. *It can't be.*

He threw down his cards and rushed from the room. Moments later, he flung open the front door just as a pair of long, shapely legs emerged from the backseat of a white limousine.

He gaped, convinced that his eyes were deceiving him. "Asha?"

A soft smile curved her lips. "Hello, Sterling."

Gazes locked, they started toward each other. When they stood face-to-face, Sterling asked, "What are you doing here?"

"I couldn't stay away," Asha confessed.

Sterling's heart lurched. "What are you saying?"

"I'm saying that I missed you. I tried to throw myself back into work, but all I could think about was this house, our children, our grandsons. *You.* I missed being here with you, Sterling. So I did the only thing that made sense. I walked out in the middle of an important meeting and ordered my pilot to fuel the jet." She smiled, tears misting her eyes. "I couldn't get here fast enough."

Sterling pulled her into a fervent embrace and kissed her as if his very life depended on it. She clung to him, her arms wrapping tightly around his neck. His heart soared.

Lifting his head, he gazed into her eyes. "I love you. I don't know when it happened, but I'm so glad it did."

"Oh, Sterling." Asha curved her hand against his cheek. "I've been in love with you since the day the twins were born."

Stunned, he stared at her. *"You have?"*

She nodded. "The way you held them in your arms and kissed their tiny foreheads while tears rolled down your face. Watching you, I was a goner. I've been trying to outrun my feelings ever since, but I can't do it anymore. I love you, and I want to be with you."

Sterling turned his face into her palm and kissed it. "What about New York?"

"I'll keep my headquarters in Manhattan and open another office in Buckhead, near the boutique."

He smiled at her decisive tone. "A woman who knows what she wants."

Asha held his gaze. "You'd better believe it."

Overcome with emotion, Sterling grabbed her hand and strode toward the house, where Michael and Marcus stood on the front steps gaping at them in disbelief.

"Help the driver carry Asha's luggage up to my room," Sterling told them gruffly.

"Yes, sir," Marcus said.

Amused, Michael drawled, "And where are you lovebirds headed?"

Sterling and Asha shared a smile. "The guesthouse."

Chapter 19

With only ten minutes left in her final appearance on *Howlin' Good,* Reese congratulated herself for maintaining her composure. She'd been on the verge of tears since she'd arrived at the studio that evening for the live taping. It hadn't helped when she'd walked onto the set and saw her parents, Raina and Warrick seated in the first row. Once she realized that Michael had arranged the big surprise for her, she'd wanted to launch herself into his arms and shower his face with grateful kisses.

She'd settled for a simple "Thank you."

His gaze had softened on her face. "I'd do anything for you."

If only that was true, she'd thought sadly.

Finished with her cooking demonstration, Reese spooned some of her curry chicken soufflé into a bowl and passed it to Michael. "Enjoy."

He arched a brow. "You mean you're not going to feed it to me?"

She rolled her eyes heavenward. "Typical helpless male."

As the audience laughed, she and Michael exchanged brief, tense smiles.

"Can I at least have a spoon?" he asked.

She heaved an exasperated breath that wasn't entirely for the crowd's benefit. After dropping a spoon into his bowl, she smiled sweetly. "Anything else?"

"Actually," he said thoughtfully, "I think I'd rather use a fork instead."

Reese scowled into the audience. "If I didn't know better, I would think he was stalling to get out of trying my soufflé."

More laughter ensued.

Muttering under her breath, Reese began searching the cluttered countertop for a clean fork.

"Try the pot on the back burner," Michael suggested.

Shooting him a dubious look, Reese lifted the lid of the pot he'd indicated. When she saw what was inside, she gasped and dropped the lid with a noisy clatter.

Her stunned gaze flew to Michael, who was smiling softly as he set down his bowl.

"Well? Aren't you going to pick it up?"

Reese opened her mouth, but no sound emerged.

Michael shook his head at the audience. "A man's work is never done."

Only a few scattered chuckles could be heard above the sudden hush that had swept over the crowd.

Michael reached inside the pot and withdrew the solitary item that had rendered Reese speechless: a small velvet box.

A collective gasp went around the room.

The expression on Michael's face was as achingly tender as his voice. "I know you're supposed to be the apprentice here, but the truth is, Reese, *I'm* the one who's been learning from you. You've taught me so much about life, love and taking chances. I promise you that I'm not the same man you met a few weeks ago."

Reese's heart swelled with emotion. "Oh, Michael…"

"My viewers and I are on the same page. I want to keep you

on the show as much as they want me to. But more importantly, Reese, I want to keep you in my life."

She stared at him, afraid to believe this moment was real.

"I love you," Michael said huskily. "You mean everything to me. *Everything.*"

Tears of joy and relief sprang to Reese's eyes. "I love you, too, Michael."

He looked deeply into her eyes, searching her soul. And then he opened the jewelry box and removed a stunning diamond ring. "In the spirit of taking chances, will you marry me?"

Smiling through her tears, Reese held out a trembling hand and felt his warm, strong fingers close tightly around hers. "Yes," she said fervently. "Yes, Michael, I'll marry you."

He eased the ring onto her finger, then yanked her into his arms and whispered hoarsely, "I love you!" before crushing his mouth to hers in a fierce, devouring kiss. The audience erupted into thunderous applause that was soon joined by laughter and whistles as the kiss continued.

Reese was oblivious to everything but Michael. In that moment, no one could tell her that she wasn't the luckiest woman in the world. How could she not be, when her favorite fantasy had just become a reality?

Hours later, Michael lay in the darkness of his bedroom with Reese cradled against his side, her head on his shoulder. His hand drifted lazily over the curve of her waist as he brushed butterfly kisses across her forehead. He couldn't stop kissing her, touching her, making love to her. Thankfully, he didn't have to. Reese wasn't going anywhere, and neither was he. *Ever.*

After wrapping up at the studio, they'd headed over to Wolf's Soul to celebrate their engagement with family and friends. Together they'd mingled with their guests, accepting congratulations and good-natured teasing about their c screen kiss, which Drew had dubbed the longest lip-lock in television history. He was already salivating at the thought of what Michael's romantic proposal had done for the show's ratings.

All Michael cared about was the woman in his arms. He couldn't help marveling at the way things had turned out. Up until a few hours ago, he'd been facing the unthinkable possibility of a future without Reese. Now, he was on top of the world.

And to think he'd almost blown it.

"I shouldn't have waited so long to tell you how I felt about you," he murmured.

"Better late than never." Reese lifted her head, searching his face in the silvery moonlight streaming through the wall of windows. "I, too, could have shared my feelings sooner, but I was so afraid you weren't ready."

"That's not what was holding me back." He touched her hair. "The day after our picnic, Marcus called to tell me about an argument he'd overheard between Mom and Grant. Apparently Mom had asked Grant if they could stay another week, and he got upset and accused her of still being in love with Dad. Marcus was stunned. He waited until no one else was around and confronted Mom. She denied Grant's accusation, but she admitted that she'd been feeling confused about the past lately. She said she loves Grant dearly, but the more time she spent with Dad, the more she realized how much she gave up all those years ago. But she promised Marcus that she'd keep her doubts to herself so she wouldn't throw Dad's life into upheaval—again."

Michael watched as comprehension dawned on Reese's face. "You thought that if your mother could have buyer's remorse after nearly thirty years, I might someday regret breaking up with Victor."

Michael hesitated, then nodded. "It killed me to think—"

"en to me," Reese interrupted, pressing a finger to his
gazing intently into his eyes. "You don't *ever* need
about me having second thoughts about us. I *love*

you, Michael Wolf. You're the only man I've ever loved or *will* ever love. So unless you wake up one morning and decide you want a new apprentice, you're stuck with me."

He smiled tenderly. "You're the only apprentice I'll ever want or need."

"Good." There was a husky catch to her voice. "Drew offered me a contract to remain on the show, but I told him I'd have to think about it. I don't mind doing cameo appearances, but as much as I've enjoyed working with you, baby, I miss being a doctor."

"Of course you do." Michael caressed her face. "You know, we have plenty of great hospitals right here in Atlanta."

"I know." She paused. "I never got around to canceling my interview at Emory University Hospital on Wednesday."

"You had an interview?"

"Yes. I'd been looking into jobs before we…" She trailed off shyly.

Michael groaned, his heart overflowing with love and gratitude as he kissed her. "What did I ever do to deserve you?"

Her eyes glimmered with mirth. "It was your triple chocolate cheesecake. Remember? You all but guaranteed it would make me fall in love with you."

He laughed. "So I did."

Smiling, she nibbled on his chin. "When can we have another picnic in the garden?"

"As soon as we can get the house to ourselves again." Reese's family was staying at Sterling's house for a week. Michael and Reese were expected to join everyone tomorrow for a festive brunch that would probably spill over into the next day. Too bad his father and Asha had dibs on the guesthouse, Michael lamented.

"I'm so excited for them," Reese murmured, as if she'd read his mind. "They look so happy together. So right for each other."

"I think they are," Michael agreed, marveling at the odds

of him and his father finding their soul mates within the same week.

"What were you and my dad discussing after dinner?" Reese asked curiously.

Michael chuckled. "He wanted to make sure I understood how precious you are to him. Before your lovely mother intervened, he mentioned something about a hunting rifle he hadn't used in years."

"Oh, Dad." Reese bit her lip, stifling a grin. "Sorry about that."

"Don't apologize. Believe me, I'm gonna be the same way with our daughters."

Her expression softened. "I promised your father that I'd give him many more grandchildren."

Michael grinned, even as his heart melted. "Many?"

"I believe that's the word I used."

"In that case," Michael drawled, rolling her over and settling between her legs, "we'd better get busy."

Reese sighed, curving her arms around his neck. "A promise is a promise."

Poised above her, Michael gazed into her eyes and saw the glorious future that awaited them. He looked forward to marrying her in the garden, then whisking her away to Italy. He looked forward to providing for her, cooking for her, nourishing her body and her soul. He looked forward to raising children with her. And he looked forward to growing old with her.

"Michael?"

"Yes, sweetheart?"

"I need you." Reese tightened her thighs around him. *"Now."*

His grin was wolfish. "One chocolate orgasm coming right up."

As he plunged into her, she threw back her head and released the throatiest, sexiest howl he'd ever heard.

Oh, yeah, Michael thought wickedly, stroking deeper. *I'm going to* love *spending the rest of my life with this woman.*

* * * * *

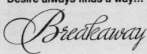

REQUEST YOUR FREE BOOKS!

2 FREE NOVELS
PLUS 2 *FREE GIFTS!*

KIMANI™
ROMANCE

Love's ultimate destination!

YES! Please send me 2 FREE Kimani™ Romance novels and my 2 FREE gifts (gifts are worth about $10). After receiving them, if I don't wish to receive any more books, I can return the shipping statement marked "cancel." If I don't cancel, I will receive 4 brand-new novels every month and be billed just $4.69 per book in the U.S. or $5.24 per book in Canada. That's a saving of over 20% off the cover price. It's quite a bargain! Shipping and handling is just 50¢ per book.* I understand that accepting the 2 free books and gifts places me under no obligation to buy anything. I can always return a shipment and cancel at any time. Even if I never buy another book from Kimani Press, the two free books and gifts are mine to keep forever.

168/368 XDN E7PZ

Name	(PLEASE PRINT)

Address	Apt. #

City	State/Prov.	Zip/Postal Code

Signature (if under 18, a parent or guardian must sign)

Mail to The Reader Service:

IN U.S.A.: P.O. Box 1867, Buffalo, NY 14240-1867
IN CANADA: P.O. Box 609, Fort Erie, Ontario L2A 5X3

Not valid for current subscribers to Kimani Romance books.

Want to try two free books from another line?
Call 1-800-873-8635 or visit www.morefreebooks.com.

* Terms and prices subject to change without notice. Prices do not include applicable taxes. N.Y. residents add applicable sales tax. Canadian residents will be charged applicable provincial taxes and GST. Offer not valid in Quebec. This offer is limited to one order per household. All orders subject to approval. Credit or debit balances in a customer's account(s) may be offset by any other outstanding balance owed by or to the customer. Please allow 4 to 6 weeks for delivery. Offer available while quantities last.

Your Privacy: Kimani Press is committed to protecting your privacy. Our Privacy Policy is available online at www.eHarlequin.com or upon request from the Reader Service. From time to time we make our lists of customers available to reputable third parties who may have a product or service of interest to you. If you would prefer we not share your name and address, please check here. ☐

Help us get it right—We strive for accurate, respectful and relevant communications. To clarify or modify your communication preferences, visit us at www.ReaderService.com/consumerchoice.

KROM10R